Time Sailors

I0527645

By Shelli Frew

Ink Smith Publishing

www.ink-smith.com

Edited by Kelsey Ferrara & Corinne Anderson
Formatted by V.J.O Gardner
Front Cover Design by Gwynn Tavares
Cover Wrap by Jose M.

Printed in the U.S.A

The final approval for this literary material is granted
by the author.

ISBN: 978-1-947578-18-0

Ink Smith Publishing
710 S. Myrtle Ave Suite 209
Monrovia, CA, 91016

For all of you.

Chapter 1 – The Last Fight

Virginia strolled around the Mission District of San Francisco on a gritty, hot summer day in 1964. She ambled, peering into shop windows and listening to the Spanish chatter that filled the street. She planned on walking to a local diner for a blackberry milkshake, but felt no hurry. The hot sun warmed the skin on her shoulders — a glorious feeling that was unthinkable in her old life. The other time seemed so long ago it was almost like a dream to her now.

People rushed by her and she watched as they stopped to chat with neighbours, flirt, and yell. The local plaza spilled over with people and life. Young men crowded the square, hollering at the hurried women walking past and several elderly gentlemen played chess with quiet contemplation. A church group milled about, listening to a priest preach about damnation and salvation. Virginia loved this time.

The old neighbourhood had been taken over entirely by immigrants from South America during the previous twenty years (a blink of an eye to a traveler), pushing the German denizens to other parts of the city. She felt so free here, *now*. No longer obligated by the rules of her time she could wear pants without consequence. She could leave her long, brown hair down or part it on the side like a man! or even chop it off. No one cared a bit.

The smell of hotdogs and french fries filled the eatery. Virginia ordered her milkshake and sat by a window, people-watching both those outside the diner and in. Teens filtered in, happily laughing and roughhousing with friends. An elderly couple sat at a booth seat, holding hands and speaking quietly. Virginia took another sip of her shake and noticed a tall, slender man watching her from across the street. He looked like a parody of a 1920's mobster: slicked back hair and pinstriped suit included. He even chewed on a toothpick, lazily rolling it around in his mouth, though Virginia could barely see it from her seat.

She paid and left the diner, intent on spending the rest of the afternoon in the park. Upon her arrival, she immediately noticed a crowd of people covered the green meadows. Mothers pushed giggling children on the swings and couples canoodled on picnic blankets. After a few hours of napping on the grass Virginia spied the man in the suit again, this time leaning against the statue of Hidalgo. He looked out over the green, his back to her, periodically taking a drag from a cigarette. The sun dipped down in the sky, bringing an evening chill that was so familiar to the city. Virginia started the trek back to her house in Twin Peaks, which was perched high on the side of the mountain. The area felt improbable to her as houses were precariously situated on cliffs, and roads were so steep the cars strained to climb them. Whoever had originally decided to build here had to have been mad. Virginia loved it. Her charming little green house, gifted to her in a letter from an older self, sat on a winding road, nestled between taller homes.

> *To: ME — Up on Corbort street. The green one with the rosemary out front. Don't forget to leave food out for the cat. He's mostly around in the 20's, 50's, and 70's. Although, I've seen him once or twice in '89. Bought the place in 1918, have it till 2065. —From: YOU*

The four-story home reminded her of an upside-down fun house. Instead of reaching up in the air, levels stacked one on top of the other; it stretched down the side of the cliff. The front door opened onto the top floor along with the kitchen and a cozy living/dining room. The first set of stairs would bring her to a small office and a library. Down the next flight: the bedrooms. And at the very bottom was a small, windowless basement where someone had written "THE DUNGEON" in messy, spiky handwriting on the door. It made Virginia smile every time she saw it. She hoped to meet whoever wrote it soon.

She had reached the outdoor staircase that cut between two buildings (a short cut up the mountain), when she heard a twig snap behind her. She spun around and peered into the twilight. She saw nothing but an empty street and turned to continue on her way. A loud pop rang out in the dark. Suddenly the man from before stepped out from the shadows on the step just above her. He wore a cold, dead look in his eyes. Virginia didn't have time to speak before the man, in one smooth, practiced motion, pulled something sharp and silver from his pocket and jammed it into her chest just below her collarbone. His other hand shot out and shoved her roughly down the stairs. She fleetingly saw the stars as she tumbled backwards to the street below. Virginia landed on the pavement, her head thumping against the hard surface. The piece of metal in her chest sent a wave of pain searing through her. The man calmly walked down the stairs towards her. She shut her eyes and willed herself elsewhen, focusing on her safe, warm home just up the hill. A jolt ran through her and she gasped. She didn't move. She tried once more and again the jolt shocked her, keeping her in the here and now. The man stepped down the last few steps, his cold eyes looking not at her, but through her.

Virginia scrambled to her feet and ran back towards the populated main streets, hoping to find people. She clutched wildly at the metal the man had impaled her with, which had only made its way deeper after the fall. Virginia, steeling herself, grabbed it and yanked it out in a quick motion. She cried out in pain and dropped it on the ground as she hurried forward, already feeling warm blood bubbling up. She ran awkwardly, cradling her wound and fighting the pain that radiated from every step. Another popping noise and the man stood in front of her, blocking her path. She stopped short, dumbstruck. He laughed, a short angry noise in the back of his throat.

He was like her!

In the roughly three-and-a-half years of her travels through time, she had never met anyone else like her. Her older self never indicated people like her existed.

In confusion she stammered, "You're the same as me."

He stopped, squinted his eyes and stared at her. "You're not her. Not yet."

He took a step towards her. Virginia felt warm blood dribbling down the side of her face and realized the fall from the stairs must have done more damage than she thought. Her heart thumped loudly in her chest as the world swirled around her, making her feel like a spinning top.

"Please."

He shook his head. "No."

He took another step. Virginia turned and ran blindly, the dizzy feeling in her head making her trip and stumble. The man's footsteps, unhurried and calm, echoed behind her. She staggered to the nearest house, a large manor surrounded by a high stone wall and a solid iron gate. Feeling her blood drench her shirt, Virginia yanked on the door handle but it wouldn't budge. She frantically rang the bell and yelled for help. The man laughed, enjoying her fear. He could easily catch her. This was just a game to him.

She sprinted away, screaming for help. No lights clicked on, no doors opened, no one came to answer her call. She turned a corner and raced down a side street. Another pop sounded, and he stood in front of her. Virginia tumbled to the ground, skinning her palms.

"Pointless to run, girl. No getting away from me."

He pulled out a knife, raked the blade over her shoulder and watched as blood welled up and trickled down her arms. She crawled forward, desperate for an escape. Virginia willed herself upright and spotted a fire escape on the next building over. She hobbled forward, as quickly as her mangled body allowed. The deep gash in her chest sent a continuous wave of pain throughout her body and the new cut on her shoulder throbbed terribly.

Virginia, somehow, made it to the ladder and forced herself upwards. Her wounds screamed in protest, but she grit her teeth and climbed, knowing her pursuer wasn't far behind. The man appeared below her almost immediately and hauled himself up.

She was reaching for the top ring of the ladder when she felt the man grip her left arm and yank her sharply back. In shock, Virginia broke her grip and they both slipped off the metal rings of the ladder and toppled towards the hard ground. Everything seemed to move in slow motion as they fell backwards. Virginia curled her right arm towards her chest and tucked her head in anticipation of the landing. The man maintained his grip on her left wrist as they fell, wrenching her arm.

In her injured mind she pictured an old manor house, far from her current city. A large, sprawling, ivy-covered home in the small mountain town where she use to live. Her sense of time muddled, she landed fifty years past when she stepped foot there previously, and ten years since anyone lived in the home. She meant to arrive on the ground floor in the parlor but instead ended up in an upstairs bedroom. She dragged the man with her through time, something she definitely did not intend to do. Virginia had never traveled with a passenger before. It was a jarring sensation that stunned her for a few seconds and drained her remaining energy, and everything went black.

****

Virginia came to lying on a dusty hardwood floor, her left arm jutted at an odd angle away from her body. It took a moment for her brain to process what she was looking at. Her left arm had sunk into the floor, just below the elbow, and in front of her the man gasped as blood sputtered from his mouth. His torso had been level with her arm when they appeared. The floor ran through him, just below where his ribs started. One arm had sunk under the floorboards, the free arm frantically clawed at the wood as he tried pulling himself free. She screamed and tugged at her trapped arm in vain as the man next to her continued to struggle.

The man's flailing grew weaker and slower until he gradually stopped raking at the floorboards. He slumped over, blood dribbling out of his mouth onto the floor. Dead.

Virginia skipped a few seconds through time and a few feet over. She peered down at her previously trapped arm. It wasn't there. Her arm ended just below the elbow, right where the floor had severed it. In confusion she grabbed the stump with her remaining hand, blood spurting through her fingers. She tried standing, fell, and tried again. The whole world wavered and her legs refused to work.

A thump of shoes echoed from downstairs. Voices shouting, then screaming. She heard several people running up the stairs before she blacked out, again.

Chapter 2 – Old New Friends

It was hot. The small house had no air conditioning, none of the houses on this block did. It was stifling everywhere; heat draped over the town, suffocating, slowing time to a crawl. Stokely rolled over, kicked the sheet off himself, and sighed. Seven in the morning and already he was covered in sweat. He rose, dressing quickly in a collared blue cotton shirt and the thinnest pants he owned. The clothes hung loose on his slim frame, an inch too short. At nineteen he stood among the tallest in his small town.

Chancy and Orsby, his roommates, sat slumped at the kitchen table fanning themselves with newspapers and eating cereal. They were having an animated discussion about the day's events.

"Yeah, getting shot's a possibility. But they know that and they *still* want to help. Why not let them?" Chancy proclaimed.

Orsby made a face. "There are worse ways to be killed than getting shot."

"What are you two arguing about?" asked Stokely, grabbing himself a bowl and sitting down.

"Dr. Belle and the nurses at his practice offered free emergency medical care for anyone injured. He's setting up shop at St. Christopher's since it's closer to where the rally is going to be than his building. He said he wanted to be close by in case anything..." Chancy paused, searching for the right word, "In case anything happens."

"What if the church gets bombed while Dr. Belle is there?" Orsby asked. "I don't see why he has to be at the church. If he gets himself killed we'll have to go an hour away to see a doctor. "

He had a point. Dr. Spatcher, the only other doctor in town, did not treat Negroes. Recently, he had begun refusing to treat whites known to sympathize with the movement.

"Well, there's nothing to be done about it now. People will do what they want to do," Stokely whispered. The three friends finished their breakfast in silence. After eating they reluctantly headed out into the oppressive heat.

Cops milled around the main streets in anticipation of the protest scheduled for that day. Upon arriving at the church the three waved to Pastor Freedman, head of St. Christopher's. It was common knowledge that this was the main church in town for the Negro community. The three also greeted Mr. Hadwin and saw that other whites were gathered around the church to march in solidarity. The friends knew Mr. Hadwin was the only one of standing. He was the owner of the only grocery store in town and a furniture factory that employed both Stokely and Orsby. He also terrified most of the children in town. Pastor Freedman and Mr. Hadwin had fought alongside each other in World War II and Mr. Hadwin bore the scars to prove it. Stokely had always been curious about the war but had never been brave enough to ask the men. It wasn't something veterans talked about.

Loads of people scurried around the back of the church. Protesters put the finishing touches on signs and shouted instructions through megaphones. Several lawyers and students from up north took down names in case of arrest. Chancy spotted his older sister, Ruth, in the crowd and led his friends over to her.

"Hello, you three. Looking for a job to do?" They nodded. "Chancy, Mr. Overby needs help at the registration booth. Orsby, Stokely you two hammer the signs together. They are in a pile around back. Thanks."

She sounded rushed and worried, although she looked perfectly put together as always: dress smooth and wrinkle free, perfect black hair tied down with a silk scarf. Ruth hurried off, leaving the scent of her rose perfume lingering in the air.

Orsby and Stokely waved goodbye to their friend and made their way to a large pile of wooden signs. Two of the student protesters were already there, busily hammering signs to wooden posts.

"Hi. I'm David and this is Stan."

"I'm Orsby. He's Stokely. Nice to meet you." They went about their work, the sweltering heat bearing down on them.

David and Stan chatted the entire time they worked, discussing their college up in Chicago. Stokely and Orsby occasionally asked them questions about campus life, but it sounded like a world that was very far from their own.

After some time, Stokely noticed a young white woman watching them. She sat under a tree at the edge of the church's land. Behind her, the woods stretched for miles and tempted Stokely with its cool shade. To say the young woman looked out of place was an understatement. All the women at the protest wore dresses and makeup with well-kept hair, while the mystery girl sported damp clothes, torn jean shorts and a button-up green men's shirt with rolled up sleeves. Half a dozen wristwatches of various size and color adorned her left arm. Her long, light brown hair hung damp around her face and she was barefoot. Next to her on the ground was a backpack and an umbrella despite the cloud-free sky. She looked familiar to Stokely, but he couldn't remember from where or when.

The young woman smiled at Stokely and waved to him. Stokely awkwardly raised his hand, sure now that he had met her before and could not remember the encounter. The other three boys turned to look at who Stokely was waving to.

"Who's that?" asked Stan.

"I don't know, but she looks familiar. Do you recognize her?" Orsby shook his head.

"I doubt she's with any of the student groups," David said. "We were told to look respectable the whole time we were here." Stokely could tell from the way he said it that David thought the girl was of an unrespectable sort.

"What if a reporter snaps a picture of her? The news will say we are encouraging vagrants." Stan nodded in agreement and Orsby shrugged his shoulders.

"Maybe she isn't here for the protest. There's a river about two miles into the woods—she might of been goin' for a swim and stopped to see what the commotion was."

Stan stared at him. "But she has shorts on. And no shoes. And I'm pretty sure that's a man's shirt. Women shouldn't dress like that, it's asking for trouble."

Stokely stood up. "Well I'm goin' to talk to her. Say hello." But as he turned, the young woman disappeared. He scanned the crowds for her but at that moment Pastor Freedman called everyone away from their assorted tasks. He stood on a chair, waving away an offered bullhorn. Years of preaching to the Sunday masses made such tools unnecessary and his deep voice soon greeted the crowd. "This is lookin' to be a long, hot, tirin' day for everyone. But, Lord willin', it will help to further our cause. I'd like to extend my thanks to everyone who came out today whether you are from St. Christopher's congregation or have traveled a great distance to get here. All of this today would not be possible if not for every one of you. Please be careful and I cannot stress this enough: keep the protest non-violent." He paused, and the crowd shifted with anticipation. "We are out to better the world. To do that we must be better than the oppressors we fight. Thank you."

The large crowd applauded and began to move as one toward the street. Stokely spotted the young woman from before. She'd somehow managed to change into a simple blue sundress during the Pastor's short speech. Her hair now looked dry and neatly brushed. Stokely wondered how she had done that. He moved through the crowd toward her, noticing that she still tread on bare feet but the umbrella and backpack were gone. The wristwatches remained and twinkled in the sunlight.

13

Coming up beside her, Stokely realized he didn't really know what to say. "Um hi—Sorry I didn't introduce myself earlier. Had to finish the signs and all." She stared at him blankly for a second before her face broke out in a wide smile.

"That's ok. Everyone's busy, right? My name's Virginia Bell." She held out her hand, which Stokely shook.

"I'm Miles. Everyone calls me by my last name, Stokely. Have we met before? You look kinda familiar."

Virginia shrugged and gave him a smile. "Who knows? Perhaps we met in a dream. You can't see the future can you? Or maybe at a circus? I've been known to travel and perform from time to time. The noblest art is that of making others happy."

The pair rounded a corner onto Haymarket Street, following the movement of the large group. Virginia stretched her arms toward the sky and continued talking. "I'm sure it's fine though. Destiny will eventually converge and right itself. Like the tide moving in and out, or a rocket ship landing on the moon."

"A rocket on the moon?"

"Well no, not yet. But it is an inevitable. Before the decade is out. Fanfare and script reading and all that." Stokely briefly wondered if Virginia was on drugs. She looked at him and smiled. "Alright ducky, I'm going that way." She pointed down a side street. "Until our paths cross again." She grabbed his hand again and shook it once.

Stokely watched her wander away. She stopped to give a flower, which was seemingly pulled from nowhere, to a delighted child. As the throng of people moved toward the main center of town, Stokely lost sight of her. The crowd walked and chanted, buzzing with energy. Stokely had never seen the town so full of life before. He spotted Orsby with a group of teens from St. Christopher's, and headed towards him.

"Orsby I saw that girl again. The one with the wet clothes," Stokely said when he caught up to his friend.

Orsby glanced at him. "Did you talk to her?"

He nodded. "Yeah, she was a trip man. She was talking about rockets and destiny and dreams."

Orsby laughed and rubbed the sweat from his forehead with a handkerchief before asking, "Is she here for the protest?"

Stokely shook his head. "I'm not sure. She says she works for a circus."

Mr. Hadwin came up suddenly beside the small group of teens. Several in the group mumbled hellos to the old man, all the while trying to avoid looking at his scarred face.

"Heard talk of police dogs being brought out," Mr. Hadwin said in his grizzled voice. "Can I count on you two boys to pass the word along?"

The boys nodded. "Of course, Mr. Hadwin," Orsby said.

The old man clapped him on the shoulder with his gnarled, fingerless hand and gave them a smile. The scars on the left half of his face twisted into more of a grimace, before he ambled away into the throng. The rest of the group looked at Orsby and Stokely with awe.

"He's not scary," Stokely said. The teens didn't argue with Stokely, but he knew none of them would change their minds about Mr. Hadwin anytime soon.

"I'll head that way and start telling people," Stokely said, pointing behind them and to the left. "You go on the other side of the street."

Orsby nodded and made his way to the right. Stokely could hear him as he left, calling out greetings to the people he knew and giving short introductions to the ones he didn't. Most of the crowd lagged behind them. As he made his way toward the back of the protesters' group, passing along greetings and warnings, he noticed a group of men standing in front of the hardware store watching the marchers. He recognized one of them as Dr. Spatcher.

Stokely wondered why they didn't join the counter-protest that was meeting in the town's main square. Out of the corner of his eye, Stokely saw a flash of sunlight that bounced off glass, calling his attention away from the men. Stokely turned to see Virginia who was once again wearing her damp clothes. He wondered why she kept changing. As he neared the tail end of the crowd, he saw his neighbors Mr. and Mrs. Green kneeling on either side of their son, Thomas. The child sat on the ground, his face pale and his breath coming in short, harsh gasps.

"Is he ok?" Stokely asked.

"He's having a fit," Mrs. Green said with a pained expression. "I think it's this heat and all the excitement."

Stokely turned to go, calling over his shoulder, "Dr. Belle's at the church. I'll run and get him. Shouldn't take me but a minute."

16

The Greens called out their thanks as he sprinted away.

The crowd was still only a few blocks from the church but by the time Stokely ran up the driveway his shirt clung to him from a layer of sweat. The heat wrapped around him like a layer of hot wool that covered his whole body. The large wooden church loomed empty and silent when he arrived. Stokely made a beeline for the back room, normally the children's room, now converted into a makeshift clinic.

"Dr. Belle! Thomas Green is sick. His mother says he had a fit.

The young, lanky Dr. Belle immediately began picking up assorted medical implements off a rough wood table that dominated the room. He put everything into a black travel bag. "Where is he?" he asked.

"On Haymarket Street just before the hardware store," Stokely answered.

Dr. Belle addressed the young woman in the room. "Alright, Jane you come with me. Young man, would you mind telling Sarah, the other nurse, where we've gone? She stepped out for a minute." Stokely nodded as the two left in a rush.

Stokely made his way to a side door that led to the church's small kitchen. His chest was still heaving from the run so he helped himself to a glass of water, then another. Standing over the sink, he heard the main door open and shut. Figuring Sarah had returned, he rinsed his cup, set it on the drying rack, and made his way back through the children's room. As he was about to turn the knob of the door handle, he heard several pairs of shoes clomping on the floor. A voice, almost too quiet for him to hear, said, "Check under the pews. You check the back. He's here somewhere. We're gonna get that nigger."

Stokely's blood ran cold and heart began to race. He peeked through a crack in the door and could barely make out Dr. Spatcher and the other men from before. As quietly as he could, Stokely flipped the lock on the door and crept back to the kitchen. He locked the kitchen door as well and gently wedged a chair under the handle, careful not to make any unnecessary noise.

The five men each had a good seventy pounds on him and Stokely doubted he could fight off one, let alone a group. He moved deeper into the kitchen and spotted a door to the basement that was partially hidden in the back of the pantry. As he carefully picked his way over cans and jars in the pantry to reach the door, a thought struck him. The nurse. If the men did not hear him leaving and stayed to search the church, what would they do to Sarah when she returned? The men began pounding on the locked door of the children's room. Stokely couldn't just run, not when there was the possibility of the men harming an unarmed woman. Men like them had certainly done it before.

Creeping back to the door before he lost his nerve, Stokely removed the chair from under the handle and unlocked the door. Just as he made his way back to the pantry, there came an almighty crash from behind him as the men broke down the door. Thinking on his feet, Stokely grabbed a large can and hurled it at the far wall. He raced down the stairs, praying that the men would investigate the commotion. He heard the men upstairs, alerted by the noise, the thumping of their shoes echoing his heart. Reaching the cellar door, he hurried to undo the dead bolt and sprinted into the bright sunshine.

He ran towards the front of the church, towards the street, towards presumed safety when the butt of a gun swung inches away from his face.

The gun's owner growled at Stokely, "Don't move!"

Stokely put his hands up. The man stepped closer to him and Stokely kicked him as hard as he could in the crotch. Better to fight dirty he figured than be dead. The man's screams caught the attention of the others and several of them came around the side of the building, blocking his exit to the street.

Stokely took off running towards the woods. The heat wrapped around him and panic flooded his body. He felt dizzy, almost like he might pass out. The men shouted behind him and Stokely could clearly hear cursing and shots being fired. A loud crack echoed through the forest and Stokely stumbled to the ground clutching his left shoulder, blood running through his fingers. Shock and pain radiated from his shoulder as Stokely stared at his blood drenched hands in disbelief. The men advanced on him as he stumbled to a small clearing. Gathered around him in a semi-circle, the men jeered. Dr. Spatcher kicked him in the stomach and another wave of laughter spouted from the men.

"You gonna die nigger." He sneered as he leveled the hunting rifle at Stokely's chest.

Stokely hated the man more than he had hated anything in his life. His whole body shook and his head spun. Spider webs of light began to bleed through his vision and he heard a loud ringing in his ears.

Another loud crack accompanied a burning pain in his chest. An icy chill flooded Stokely's body and he fell backwards. He felt something wet and cool seeping into his thin cotton shirt. Stokely's whole body ached and he thought to himself, if this was dying, it isn't so bad.

Then he fainted, dead away.

Some time later, Stokely groggily opened his eyes. He lay on his back in the forest, but everything looked wrong. Staring up at the suddenly leafless trees, he saw the setting sun peeking out from behind wispy clouds. Snow, fresh and new, covered the forest. A strange, purple cloth was wrapped around him. It felt incredibly soft, and seemed to radiate heat. It also appeared dry despite laying over the fresh snow. His shirt sat neatly folded next to him and someone had bandaged his shoulder, which throbbed dully.

Stokely scanned the trees, alerted by a sudden noise. The strange girl from the rally—Virginia, he recalled—appeared, her arms loaded with sticks. A piece of purple fabric, much like his own, was draped over her shoulders. Her feet were still bare even in the blistering cold.

She arranged the wood in a pile. "Sorry I had to take your shirt off. How's your shoulder?"

Stokely ran his hand over the bandage and wiggled his shoulder a bit. "It's fine, I think. Doesn't hurt."

She smiled broadly at him and pulled a small grey ball out of her pocket. Tugging on a black string attached to the ball, she pulled it loose and tossed it into the pile of sticks. Instantly, it burst into flames.

"Um…where am I?"

"Exactly where you're meant to be, I imagine. The same place as before. North America. The Earth. Pick whichever answer you like."

Stokely frowned at her. "It's snowing," he said with a look of confusion. "Am I dead?"

Virginia threw her head back and laughed a loud, unapologetic laugh. "I thought you were too calm for someone in such a strange situation, ducky. You've been operating under the assumption you were dead, huh? Well, don't worry, you're not. Almost were, though. Don't think I've ever seen such a close shot before." She pointed to his chest where a small Band-Aid rested right over his heart. "You saved your own skin though. That'll make an impressive story. And why on Earth would the afterlife have snow?"

Virginia spread her own purple cloth on the ground and sat down cross-legged. She looked at Stokely like a small child waiting for an answer.

"Because hell is hot? And I don't think I went there, so this must be heaven—the opposite of hell? I don't know."

"That's a fair enough answer, I'd say. The hottest place in Hell is reserved for those who remain neutral in times of great moral conflict. And you certainly weren't remaining neutral, were you?"

Virginia paused to watch a bird take flight off a nearby branch. Smiling, she turned back to Stokely. "Well, would you like to know what happened?"

He nodded.

"Alright I want you to imagine a life. What do you think it looks like?"

This was not the answer Stokely was looking for. "A life? What? I dunno, a road or line I guess?"

"Of course. We begin at the beginning: birth, childhood, adolescence, as awkward and uncomfortable as it is, adulthood with all its toils and joys, old age if we are lucky, and at the end, death. Tied to our own lines of life is time as it is around us." She moved her hands often as she spoke, weaving them around, and making grand gestures. "Time: a commodity, a nuisance, a privilege, and a shared aspect of life. Everyone experiences it roughly the same, yes? Here in America it's 1965, by the Persian calendar it's 1334, Hijri Calendar 1384 but it's still the same time for all of us, yes? Yes. Sometimes time seems to go faster or slower depending on our circumstances. But..." She leaned toward Stokely, a glint in her eyes. "But I don't follow the line with everyone else. And you don't have to either. I like to think everyone is on their own boat moving on a current that only allows them one path. Time is the water moving under them, pulling them forever one way. Sometimes faster, sometimes slower. But I, and now you my dear Stokely, dove off our respective boats into the water. We can swim against the current as we please."

Stokely rubbed his hands over his short-cropped hair, a nervous gesture. Virginia was insane. She must be.

"Are you understanding me, Stokely? You moved through time. Quite well, I must say. Only six months from when you left off. First time I traveled I shot myself a hundred years. Wouldn't recommend that the first time. Too confusing."

Stokely stared at her. "You're off your rocker."

She giggled. "You're the one sitting in the middle of a snowy clearing. It was summer a bit ago, yes? Where did the summer go?" Stokely opened his mouth to give an answer, and then realizing he had none, closed it. He stared at the strange young woman before him.

Where had the summer gone?

"Why haven't you got shoes on? You must be freezing."

Virginia uncrossed her legs and wiggled her toes.

"It's a clear thermo-membrane. Think of it as an incredibly strong metal mixed with the warmest wool, turned into a clear liquid that's sprayed on a body. Strong, warm, or cool depending on what you need. Water proof, fire proof. From quite some time in the future."

"You're from the future then?"

She smiled at him and shrugged. "You hungry? Of course you are, hunger is inevitable."

The comment made Stokely think of their earlier conversation. As Virginia rummaged through her backpack he peered at her intently. "You said that before. That something was an inevitable. What did you mean by that?"

Virginia paused and glanced at him with a quizzical look. "I did? When?"

"Just as the march started. When you changed into that blue dress."

She furrowed her brow. "Blue dress? Oh, ok, I think I remember. You apologized for not saying hello or something?"

"Yes. And you were talking about rockets on the moon. Does that really happen?"

Virginia smiled. "Sure does. Well, an inevitable, huh? When I say that I mean something that will, must, and always happen. Really, everything ever. We move through time in an odd manner but everything still happens as it happens. We don't change history anymore than we could influence the future outside of what has already happened. The ocean of time is always there, always has been. For example, the me you met, the one in the blue dress, was a younger me. I went through a history phase for a while- would go participate or watch all the important moments in history. When you came up to me, I realized I must have greeted you in your past at some point in my future. It was an inevitable. We don't change time; it is just a different less linear experience for us. So I knew older me would eventually greet you, causing you to later talk to younger me. See? An inevitable."

She handed him a sandwich. "Alright, assuming you're not crazy and I'm not dead or in a mental hospital, why are we able to travel through time?"

Virginia shrugged. "Not sure. I've heard lots of theories from other travelers. Some people think we are decedents of time travelers from the future. A while from now people start building real, working time travel machines. These travelers aren't like us. They have to use their devices which take fuel and crazy insane math calculations and sometimes they don't even take them to the right when. So, some people think those travelers go back in time and shack up with someone not of their time and have kids. And maybe because half of our genetics are out of time, time travelers like you and me are born. Except, our parents have parents and brothers and sisters and other family so where did all those people come from? Maybe the original time displaced ancestor was farther back and the travel bit only comes out once in a great while. Like browned eyed parents with browned eyed parents all of a sudden having a blue-eyed baby. Do you like the sandwich? It's from my favorite shop in 1996."

Stokely nodded. He was getting used to her unusual way of talking and found her fast hand motions less distracting.

"How did you know my name if you only just remembered meeting me a long time ago? Or I just met you from a long time ago?"

Virginia smiled at him and said, "You're sharp, Stokes. I've seen you a couple a times recently. Once at the ocean, another time at an amusement park. And most recently a rainy night next to a lake. You told me we would meet at the smallest protest I had been to in the 60's, which was the one in your town. Apparently you and me go on some awfully grand adventures. Here, you even gave me this."

She pulled a small bronze star shaped medallion attached to a blue and yellow cloth. On one side was the relief of an eagle holding lightning bolts. She handed it over to Stokely who took it gingerly with both hands, as if it was made of glass.

He held the medallion to his chest and gave her an unsettled look. "So I have to go with you?"

Virginia shook her head. "No one has to do anything—except die, eventually. You do as you please. And I will do as I please, which right now is to go to a carnival in the 1920's. If you're done with your sandwich you are more than welcome to come with me."

Stokely shook his head, annoyed with her answer. He slipped the medallion into his pocket as he said, "No. You said you met me and I told you to meet me. Or maybe you told me to tell you to meet me. I can't not do something if I've already done it, right?"

Virginia frowned. "I've never thought of it that way. I see it more as all of us, all people and animals and even plants, are constantly making little tiny insignificant decisions along with the big life-altering ones. Everything we do, whether you think it's important at the time or not, changes the world around you. For most, it's cause and effect: they make a decision, act on it, and see the results of what they did. Sometimes we see our results before we are aware we have a choice on something, because of the way we experience time. That doesn't mean you have any less free will than anyone else. You just have more direct insight into the outcomes of any given situation."

"Couldn't I go back and change something if I wanted? Maybe stop myself from going to the march so I never meet you and we never travel together?"

Virginia shook her head, "I've tried to change things. Many times. You're welcome to try but it never works. Smarter people than you and I have puzzled over why time is unchangeable. We could go visit some of them, ask what they have found out."

"What if… what if no one remembers when something is changed? Even the person doing the changing?" Stokely asked, still not fully understanding.

"What if the oceans turn to ash and we all learn to fly? Does it matter? If you really could change things you might turn the world into something unrecognizable, into something horrible. People play the what-if game their whole lives but it's not a game anyone's going to win. Perhaps people have changed things and we don't remember what it was before. Perhaps every time someone tries to change something it splits the world in two, makes a new one we can't see or touch. Maybe that happens for all the choices we make and there are millions and millions of what-if worlds out there. Could be there's a world where you died, a world where I'm a Queen, a world where everyone uses shoes as money."

Stokely laughed. "You go off on tangents a lot, you know that?"

She smiled. "I may have been told that before. It's sort of my code for life. Become a living tangent. Or maybe be so mixed up that no one can pin me down as any one thing."

"Sounds like an exciting life."

"Of course it's exciting! I get to be a pirate, a cowboy, and an astronaut all in the same week. Well, not the same week but relative to me, a week. That's what the universe is offering you, an exciting life full of mystery and adventure!"

The notion intrigued him but he remained unconvinced.

"That may be alright for you, but I have responsibilities to see to. I want to see how the march went and check on that nurse. And my family will wonder what happened to me."

Virginia waved away his concern as if it were no more than a speck of dust. "The march went fine, the nurse is fine, it's all fine. You can *time travel*. What part of that are you having trouble comprehending, Stokeadoke? You can travel with me or without me for as long as you want and go right back to when you were when you're done. For the rest of your life: journeying and questing one day, normal the next."

"That's how you live your life, then?"

"Goodness no. At least not right now. Maybe years from now it will change and I'll go back to when I'm from. But for right now I'd rather be a perpetual motion machine."

"Don't you think your family will notice you've aged years overnight?"

She grinned mischievously. "How old do you reckon I am?"

Stokely shrugged. "Maybe 19 or 20? Around my age."

She consulted her watches, in particular a purple one set nearest her hand. "I'm around about 326, although that's not exact."

He laughed at her. "I don't believe that for a second. Come on, how old are you really?"

"Really? I'm not sure. This watch," she touched the purple one, "keeps track of my heart rate. Knows the average number of beats I get in a day's time. It uses that to figure out, approximately, how old I am. I didn't start wearing it 'til sometime after I started traveling and it gets confused sometimes when my heart rate goes up or down too much. I've got a timer set as well but it gets screwy all the time. Other travelers have told me they get themselves carbon dated but I think they're kidding."

"How could you possibly be that old?"

"Science, my friend. It works. Something called nanotechnology. Keeps me young and healthy for an obscene amount of time. You can stay eternally young as well if you want. Most travelers partake at some point."

"Most travelers. Just how many are there? Is it like some kind of club with rules and…and dues and meetings?"

Virginia knelt by the fire, scooping up snow and dumping it over the dying flames. "I've met lots, mostly at parties and parades. Places odd-looking folks will blend in. If you ever aren't sure where or when to go, try to end up near San Francisco or Halloween, whichever is easier. People won't bat an eye if you look out of time. There aren't really that many travelers, but we have a habit of finding each other. There are some sorta-kinda rules, like everyone can travel forwards and backwards only so much, but everyone is different. Some can travel hundreds and hundreds of years, some only a few decades. Also some people have better aim, I guess you would say. I can show up within a few minutes of when I want, some people days, some more. But that I think has more to do with practice than anything else. We move through time as well as space but everyone is better at one then the other. You'll figure out yours after a while, but I figure it'll be time you're better with since you showed up here at the same spot you were shot. Some can travel halfway around the world in the blink of an eye. It's a pretty nifty trick."

Stokely thought about this for a minute. "Can you prove it? Right now, go to a different time—" No sooner had the words left his mouth, the woods echoed with a sudden crackling noise, like electricity. Another Virginia appeared, identical to the one already present except sans her purple cloth. Swirling snowflakes filled the air around the new Virginia.

The two looked at each other and smiled identical smiles. They glanced at Stokely and said in unison, "How's that for a magic trick?" Both laughed at Stokely's stunned expression.

He stood, walking over to the pair. Slowly he reached out with both hands, placing one on either girl's face, as if trying to assert that they were both real. They shivered at his icy fingers. The original Virginia grabbed his hand, held it in her own.

"You're freezing!" she said. The original Virginia led him back to his blanket, gently but firmly pushing onto it and wrapping her own blanket around his shoulders.

The new Virginia sat on the ground opposite Stokely, rubbing her temples with her hands. "You better get on soon. I'm starting to feel all swimmy."

Stokely asked, "Are you alright?"

Nodding, she answered, "Yeah, it's just, after being around your younger self for too long it makes a body feel strange. Kinda like your head is wrapped in cotton, or you've taken a lot of cold medicine, or like you need to throw up. Not really sure why."

New snow started to fall, large swirling flakes lazily drifting toward the ground. The original Virginia leaned over Stokely and gave him a small peck on the cheek.

"Bye for now."

Stepping back from him, the air crackled, same as before, and she was gone. The air around her became momentarily devoid of falling snowflakes before more filled the space. The other Virginia sat on the ground, scooping snow with her hands, forming it into snowballs. She stacked the small globes into miniature snowmen. Looking over at Stokely she said, "Well that was something, eh?"

She stood, brushed off her hands and walked over to Stokely. Looking down at him with her hands on her hips she said, "So it's up to you Stokes. What's it going to be? Ordinary or adventure? Live a linear life or will you go swimming with me in the sea of time?"

Stokely contemplated it for a second. "How about we go watch a rocket land on the moon instead of the carnival?"

Virginia smiled and winked. "How about a compromise, ducky? Let's go to a carnival on the moon."

Chapter 3 – Meeting New People

Sam dreamed the same dream she's had since she was a little girl.

It's summer, which means America, wide-open fields, and long hot nights sleeping in the screened-in front porch. The dream brings her back to Nan and Pop's farm. Mom's long hair in a French braid, her pale face and arms turning tan to match Sam's skin. She swims down at the river by the edge of the farm. It begins to rain big fat drops, warm and comforting like an old friend. She knows her mom will come find her soon. There could be lightning, she will say, with an edge of fear in her voice, there could be flooding, there could be snakes. She is only a little girl and she already understands her mother is full of fear. Perhaps she has taken all Sam's fear for herself because Sam is never afraid.

Time passes, the water grows colder and the light dims. She wonders where her mother is. Why she hasn't called her back to the big white farmhouse, yet? Behind her the shadows are long, creeping over the fields and the woods. Twigs snap and suddenly there is a man standing before her at the edge of the water. It's her father at first, same lanky limbs as her, same curly hair, his dark skin glistening with a sheen of rainwater.

Then the dream changes.

Now it is a different man, this one full of anger and rage. His teeth are long sharp points that he gnashes together. He might be the big bad wolf. Sam tries to swim away from him, to the other side of the river, but he is faster. He grabs her, holds her underwater. She can't break free, can't yell for help. Thrashing about, she sucks in water.

Sam is afraid.

****

Sam jerked awake, thrashing, coughing out water that wasn't there. She lay on the floor under the kitchen table—sleepwalking again. Sighing, she sat up and rubbed her arm where she had knocked it against the leg of the table, a bruise was already forming. The lights shone brightly above her, having been activated when she sleepwalked around the room.

She shakily got to her feet, still spooked from the nightmare. She felt foggy, as though she was half dreaming and half awake. Sam looked around her small one-room studio apartment, reassuring herself that she was home in Bath. In the U.K. and not on her grandparents farm. Here, the orderly kitchen area, everything neatly put away. Here, her bed, sheets rumpled from sleep, blanket pulled onto the floor. Here, her desk with her computer and desktop 3-D printer. Here her small book collection carefully alphabetized in the shelves above.

The alarm on her laptop dinged 5:30 A.M and began playing quiet music as her home woke up around her. The light next to her bed turned on gradually growing brighter. The teakettle, receiving an order from the computer, turned itself on.

Hunting through her dresser she found her favorite bathing suit, a blue one-piece with a silver stripe down the middle. It was a smart suit that was able to monitor her heart rate, how fast she swam, and how many laps she completed. She put the suit on along with an old pair of jeans and her blue running shoes.

The kettle whistled at her. Tea to start her day. Today was Tuesday, which meant toast and a protein shake for breakfast. After that, she'd go for a run, about two kilometers, and fifty laps in a swimming pool. Always a set routine for her, a holdover from her childhood. The rest of the day would be spent working on campus at the City of Bath College, down in the basement of the Music and Performing Arts Building. A large assortment of books was recently gifted to the college and took up most of Sam's time at work. Most people would probably find the job of sorting through the specialized collection lonely, but Sam enjoyed the quiet.

She ran through the cool, but not cold, air; the rain of the previous week had finally let up. Arriving at the public pool, Sam noticed two people on the walking path out front. A tall (although not quite as tall as Sam), lanky, dark-skinned young man sat on the wide steps that led to the front doors of the building. The other, a pale young woman without shoes, crouched on the sidewalk as she drew with chalk and explained something to the man. He looked at his friend with confused amusement on his face.

When Sam approached the pair she could hear the woman say in a thick, American accent, "See here, this shows the rate of expansion. If they didn't have this, they could end up in empty space. And here shows the wobble of the earth, 'cus the circle around the sun isn't ever a perfect circle. See? We don't have to worry 'cus we just know this stuff. Understand?"

The man laughed a bit and answered back in an equally thick American accent, "Not really."

As Sam started to climb the stairs she glanced back to look at the woman, who smiled up at her with a toothy grin. A smile Sam's mother would say was full of mischief.

Inside, the building stood empty of people except for the janitor, a kind old Scottish man who had worked there since Sam was a child. He waved to her as she walked toward the lap pool. She loved the pool this early in the morning since she had the whole place to herself. She embraced the shock of the cold water on her skin as she slid under the surface. She reveled in the feeling of weightlessness and power, and soon she was shooting back and forth through the pool. It was her own kind of private meditation: arm forward, head turn, breathe, legs kick, and repeat.

She left her waterproof headphones in her bag, instead concentrating on the sound of the splashing water. Her smart suit made a loud ping noise when she hit 50 laps, a high shrill note she could hear over the churning pool. Knowing she would be early to her work anyway, Sam allowed herself a few minutes of relaxation. She floated on her back in the water, staring up at the ceiling.

Sam climbed out of the pool and walked barefoot to the women's locker room, leaving a trail of water behind her. She fumbled for the light switch. The old buildings still had dumb electronics that couldn't work themselves and needed to be turned on manually. It made Sam feel slightly out of time, as if she had slipped through a wormhole into the past. The building had been constructed so long ago, when her grandmother was still a child. Sam sometimes studied pictures of Gran Dewhurst swimming there. The photos began with her as a young girl, her long hair in cornrows and a smile plastered on her face in every frame. Later pictures showed an awkward teen with arms folded defiantly over her chest and a scowl aimed at the camera. The building in those photos had remained the same to this day. Sam sometimes felt she might run into a young version of her Gran, she could catch her swimming in the pool or gossiping in the locker room.

Sam peeled off her wet suit, tossing it into the quick dryer, another simple machine she switched on manually. She turned on the hot water until it was almost scalding. As she scrubbed herself she heard happy shrieks of laughter coming from the warm leisure pool. It appeared she was no longer alone.

Sam toweled off and pulled her clothes on. She ran her fingers through her dark curly hair and rubbed lotion onto her skin, already tan and sure to darken over the summer. Walking through the building, Sam peeked her head into the hall containing the warm pool to see who made the commotion. It was the pair from before. The young woman swam in the pool fully clothed and the young man sat off to one side reading a paperback book with his feet dipped in the water. The young woman climbed out of the pool and immediately jumped back in, sending a spray of water over her companion. The man covered the book with his arms. It was rather funny to see someone so young with a paperback, especially near the water. Sam wondered why he didn't have an e-reader, most of them were waterproof now.

Sam turned and walked out into the sunshine

She enjoyed the short walk to her work. Once she arrived at the large square art building, she scanned her I.D. bracelet to get inside. Maggie, the secretary on duty, greeted her with a sleepy hello. The only students in the building at this hour were the dancers: long, leggy boys and girls in tights and leotards. She could hear them bounding around on the second floor just above her head.

Sam headed to the basement, a large room with rows and rows of books that always smelled slightly musty. The lights blinked on as she started her descent down the stairs, shutting each of them off as she went into her workspace to conserve energy. She stood in the middle of the basement, the stairs like a dark, gaping mouth of black. Sam turned her back and headed to the far corner where her workspace waited. There stood a small desk upon which sat her computer, a little printer, and her book scanner. The scanner, an incredibly sophisticated machine, greatly simplified her job. Sam clicked on some music from the computer before starting her work. The Peaceful BullD's, her favorite band, filled the room.

Sam grabbed a book off one of the many stacks that surrounded her and glanced at the cover: Joseph

Cornell. Although she could catalog books with her eyes closed, the scanner worked much faster. She held the book to the camera lens on the scanner until it flashed a green light and the cover appeared on her computer screen. A wheeled cart, already half full of books destined for the artist biography section, rolled over to her. She worked quickly and managed to catalogue about a hundred books in an hour. The computer knew the location of odd books Sam would have to look up: The Human Form and Electrical Stimulants by L. Armstrong, Gravity as a Supplement by Hank Green, How to Learn Ballet in Space by Mary Roach.

But of course the machine wasn't perfect. Every once in a while she stumped it with a very old, very rare find. Such books were sent to the restricted section of the small library where they would be housed behind glass and handled with the utmost care. A wide range of publications found their home here: original prints of books not in circulation anymore, large bound artist prints, one of a kind notebooks filled with doodles and writings by long dead painters and dancers. These she tended to carefully, with gloves on, wrapping the books in felt. Sam loved these old books, these secret treasures she discovered.

After about three hours of work she accumulated several carts filled with books to be shelved. She headed to the building's elevator, a very old box that was rarely used by anyone, as it hadn't been upgraded with the rest of the building. It couldn't sense when someone was waiting and instead needed a button to be pushed to summon it. It also couldn't tell when to close its doors, but randomly shut on people's arms or legs. Of course it opened back up when it touched them, but it still scared some people. The book carts trailed behind her like obedient dogs, crowding into the elevator with her. The short, claustrophobic trip took her to the third floor, to the sun-bathed library. The book carts went their separate ways, waiting patiently for her in different sections.

She worked her way around the large stacks, shelving the books as she walked. Students filtered into the room and occasionally asked her help with the location of a particular text. Sam rounded a corner and could suddenly hear Mrs. Veda, the ancient Head Librarian, giving a lecture to a class of freshman in one of the conference rooms. At one point a soft-spoken blond-haired, brown-eyed woman asked for help locating an Aztec art book. Her companion, a tall man with a port wine stain on his cheek, browsed the books on textiles while the pair talked.

About two hours later, Sam finished with the regular books and made her way to the restricted section. She waved her I.D. bracelet toward the glass doors, which silently slid open for her. The smell of old paper and cloth floated through the air as she entered the small room. The shelves here held fewer books. Some of the most fragile texts lived in their own special glass cases that only opened with an old-fashioned, physical key. Old maps and important papers hung on the walls, entombed in a sturdy plastic resin.

In the corner of the room there loomed the combination information storage reader and archive scanner, a machine Mrs. Veda had recently taught Sam to use. Sam started her work here. She carried a box filled with old microfilm reels, aperture cards, and microfiche sheets to the desk and sat down in front of the imposing contraption. To her left was the reader, set up to receive any kind of storage device (from the fragile microcards made of cardboard to magnetically sensitive floppy disks to old USB flash drives). Directly in front of her sat the computer. To her right was a large scanner, capable of copying the contents of whole books in an instant. It sometimes had trouble with handwritten materials, possibly where the writer pressed lightly onto the paper and the scanner couldn't pick up what was written. This would result in error messages that flashed on the computer screen and the long, mundane work of scanning individual pages.

Sam fed reels of film into the machine. Text and images popped up on the computer screen and were then saved as a digital copy. The reader was a cumbersome machine, but it worked fast. Sam finished the large box in half an hour. Next, she moved to the books. While every rare book had a digital counterpart for students to use, it was rare they were permitted to handle an actual text. Sam put on gloves and picked up a book, a first edition of signed prints by Sally Mann. She, very gently, sat it on the scanner, which looked like a very strange square-shaped bowl. She brought the top of the scanner down until it completely encased the book and then pressed the start button. She could see a bit of green light bleeding through around the edges where the scanner was slightly open. The machine beeped at her, alerting her that the process was complete. She carefully took the book out of the scanner and compared the physical copy to the digital twin that appeared on the computer screen. A perfect copy.

****

Sam checked the time and saw that she had just a few minutes before her lunch break. She decided to spend that time leafing through the book in her hands, instead of scanning more. She was ahead of schedule anyway, Sam told herself. The book was split into four sections, starting with "At twelve." She turned to this section. Young girls in a black and white photograph greeted her. A girl smiling at the camera with a mouth full of metal, perhaps old style braces, a tiny girl lying on a bed next to a baby in a room full of china dolls, and Sam wondered if they were sisters. She flipped the page, and saw a tomboyish girl next to a short man. This photo bothered Sam for some reason. The two touched like father and daughter, her arm casually thrown over his shoulder, but there remained space between them. The girl's other arm slid off the side of the picture almost as if she wanted to escape.

Her I.D. bracelet chirped at her, telling her to go on break. She set the book back on the cart and made her way out of the room.

Mrs. Veda sat typing at the main computer when Sam walked up to the information desk.

"Hello Sam. Break time for you, yes?" Sam loved Mrs. Veda's accent. She was a plump little Indian woman who had grown up on the Ivory Coast in Africa. This gave her a throaty, almost French voice. She often wore saris made from cheerful cloth from Africa and always painted her nails in vibrant colors.

Mrs. Veda seemed to be under the impression that Sam was terribly underweight because she was always trying to feed her.

"Yeah. I'm almost done with the rare collections. I've left the cart in the room. Can I get you a coffee or something while I'm out?"

Mrs. Veda shook her head, "No thank you. Have some of my paneer if you want. It's in the staff fridge."

Sam thanked her and left the building. She headed for the pie shop across the street to pick up some lunch. A bell chimed when she walked through the door and the smell of warm dough enveloped her. She ordered several pies to go, two black beans with vegetables and one with bacon and tomato. The weather was so lovely she decided to eat on the roof. She walked up the five flights of stairs and opened the door with a wave of her I.D. bracelet and a combination that she entered into a lock. The second lock was fairly new, installed after security found out students had figured out how to confuse the I.D. scanners into unlocking.

It was warm on the roof so Sam sought shelter in the shade of a solar catcher. These enormous, thick metal poles stood several meters tall and had solar arrays perched on top, which casted long shadows below. The arrays looked like giant black leaves spiraling towards the sun in clusters. She headed to the far side of the roof, where she knew a staff member stashed several folding chairs. Just as she made her way around the corner of the air conditioner, she heard voices.

"Yeah, well, you could have told me that before. You kinda lied to me."

"I never lied! I just didn't know it would be so hard for you. I really think you just need more practice. And anyway I can just take you back, no problem."

"I have been practicing! We've been all over! If this is gonna work I gotta be able to move around and do my own thing sometimes."

Sam stepped out from behind the air conditioner. It was the pair she had seen at the pool earlier. "How did you two get up here? Only staff are permitted on the roof," Sam demanded.

The two looked at each other before the woman spoke. "Well, we're doing a project on the advancements in solar energy and its efficiency in habitually cloudy areas, so we came up to look at the arrays."

The lie was so quick and so smooth Sam almost believed it.

"The science building has arrays open to the public. Also student I.D. bracelets, which I can see neither of you are wearing, can't open the door and you would need a combination for the other lock which, is only given to staff. You two aren't staff."

"You seem kinda young to be staff at a college," the young woman remarked.

"And you seem rather barefoot and unidentifiable to be a student. You should have your I.D. bracelet on at all times."

The three of them stood looking at each other for a minute before the young man spoke up. "Um. We're real sorry. We don't have ah... solar," he waved toward the arrays, apparently unsure what they were called. "Solar towers where I'm from and I wanted to see some up close. We didn't know the science building had some open to the public."

Sam raised an eyebrow at him. "How did you get the door open?"

The woman pulled a small leather case out of her pocket and opened it. Inside were several thin metal rods, each with a slightly differently shaped tip. "It's a lock-picking kit. I'm in the circus, you know escape from handcuffs and chains and stuff. I'm Virginia."

Sam knew she should call security up there to kick them out but the lock-picking kit intrigued her.

"Can you really open doors with those?"

Virginia nodded and held the kit out to her. Sam took it from her. The leather of the case felt soft and worn. She studied the small tools, touched the light delicate metal. Virginia pointed out a small, plastic, child-sized ring embedded with wires and computer chips so tiny she could barely see them. This, she explained to Sam, contained a scanner that confused any automated door that wanted an I.D., much like a skeleton key.

The church across town chimed the half hour. "You two should go, the security guard always comes up to smoke around this time."

Virginia grabbed a bag off the ground and quietly headed toward the door. Sam could see the bottoms of her feet were very dirty. "Hey wait, your kit."

Virginia waved a hand at her. "Keep it. I've got others. It might be useful to you."

The young man stuck out his hand to her, "I'm Stokely by the way. Don't mind Virginia, she's about as odd as they come." Sam shook his hand and he too walked back to the door. She heard it slam shut behind them.

She ate her lunch while talking with Beck, the security guard. He was a big man with a burly mustache who smoked cigarettes that he rolled himself. The smell reminded her of her father.

After eating she went back to the library, intent on finishing the cart of rare books before the day was over. The first few books were scanned easily, but she had trouble with the fourth one. It was an album of a dance company in France. The odd text contained individual pictures that were wrapped in clear plastic. On the back of the photographs, in small handwriting, was information too small for the scanner to pick up. Sam began the arduous task of scanning each picture, one at a time, with a small handheld scanner. She wondered about the girls in the pictures. They were all dressed nicely, long skirts and beehive hairdos. She found a date on the back of one picture: 1967. Her grandparents would have been children when these were taken. The pictures spanned several years, the hairstyles changed, the girls changed. Toward the back of the book, in what she judged to be around 1970 or so, Sam found a picture that almost made her drop the album.

It was in a rehearsal room, not a stage. There were seven young women lined up at a bar next to a row of mirrors. They were all smiling and several seemed in the middle of laughing, their mouths open wide, their eyes crinkled. Third from the back in the line of dancers was a woman who looked like Sam. The same angular face, the same curly hair, the same tan skin. It was impossible.

Sam quickly scanned the page into the computer. She brought the picture up on the screen and told the computer to translate it from French, which she could speak but not read, into English.

"Dance rehearsal. Everyone warming up. Three weeks to show time. Mademoiselle Curie {Unable to read} dancers."

There were no names written on the picture. Sam stared at the photo for several minutes. Could it be a family member? She thought about her dad's family. It had to have been someone related to her father, as Sam looked nothing like her mother aside from her eyes. She flipped to the end of the album and found two more pictures with the woman. She quickly scanned them and brought up the translations on the computer.

The first one was a large group of women in a dressing room. They were in various states of dress, some wearing costumes, some pulling on dresses or skirts. Several were standing in front of a mirror putting on makeup. Sam's doppelganger was closest to the camera, reaching her hand out to take a rose from a man. The man had his back turned toward the camera, but Sam could see he was wearing the pants of a Thai fisherman. The translation of the back read, "getting ready for the big night. Full house. Boy from {Unable to read} brought flowers for head dancers."

The other picture showed the woman with a much older lady in the rehearsal room. The older woman's hair was tied into a tight bun and she had a stern look about her. She was lightly touching the woman's chin with one hand and pointing toward the air with the other. The young woman had a look of concentration on her face, balanced on the tips of her toes with her arms up over her head. She was looking straight into the camera. She could have been Sam's twin.

The words written on the back were clear enough to be fully translated, "Mademoiselle Curie gives private instructions to Rose. 1969."

There was a whoosh of air as the door opened. Mrs. Veda walked in, smiling at Sam as she said, "Just need to get some books for a class. How is it going in here?"

Sam stared a little, open-mouthed, at her before answering, "I'm in this book."

Mrs. Veda walked over to her frowning. She put on her reading glasses and peered at the screen. "Why, she looks just like you. Amazing. Does it say who she is?"

Sam shook her head. "It's got the first name only. Rose. I don't know her."

"Perhaps it is family you have never met. You should copy it; go ask about it later, yes?"

Sam nodded. "Yeah, I'll do that. Thanks for the suggestion."

Mrs. Veda smiled at her. The old woman gathered several books and headed out the door with a little wave. Sam sent copies of the pictures to herself.

She busied herself with scanning the remaining books, but her mind kept wandering back to the mysterious pictures. Who was that woman? Sam wondered what it would be like to dance on a stage in front of an audience. She wondered what show the woman was preparing for.

At four p.m., Sam had finished her work. She tidied the room and said goodbye to Mrs. Veda before heading out. As she was walking out of the building Sam waved goodbye to Beck, who was sitting at the security guard's desk near the front doors. She made her way to the gym, where she had a dance class. In addition to the structured way she was raised that had carried into her adult life, Sam maintained a daily, strict regimen of exercise. It was a vestige from her stepfather, a professional athlete in his youth who had instilled a love of physical activity in her. Sam enjoyed the two-hour workout, which consisted of a class that combined ballet, break dancing, and martial arts. She was happily tired by the time it ended.

The walk back to her house was pleasant, the day cooling off. Sam steamed some vegetables, grilled some chicken, and made a salad for her dinner. She listened to music by Bone-chachie and the Pixters and read a few chapters from J. Scribble's newest book, Best Wishes: A Memoir, while she ate. After dinner she washed the dishes in the small sink. The light outside had begun to dim and the sky filled with soft oranges and reds. While her hands were submerged in the warm water the computer began chirping and said: "Call from your mother. Call from your mother."

As she turned to tell it to answer she accidentally knocked over her drinking glass. It fell to the floor and shattered. The noise surprised Sam and made her heart jump.

Suddenly the world tilted. Sam could smell sawdust and oranges. There was a hitch in her lungs as if she had been running, and a buzzing in her ears. All at once it felt as if someone had shoved her, hard, right in the chest.

She staggered a bit.

The room looked different.

She was standing next to her bed. The sink was empty, there was no broken glass on the floor and it was bright outside, the sun no longer in the midst of setting.

The clock on her computer said 6:34 A.M. Sam stood very still, feeling slightly shell-shocked. Slowly she lowered herself to the floor and drew her knees to her chest. She was trying hard not to panic. How had she gotten to the other side of the room? Why was it morning? Sam sat, staring at her hands. After several minutes of this she eventually noticed her hands were still wet from the dishwater. In fact there was a filmy residue from the dish soap on them. She got up and numbly washed the soap off. She sat at her computer, thinking. She should call someone for help. Her parents, or emergency services.

Sam glanced at her computer screen and froze. It said Tuesday. May the 20th, 2031, Tuesday at 6:47 A.M. Which was impossible. It had already been the 20th of May. Her computer was wrong. She opened one of her daily newsfeeds, *The Times*. It said the same thing, May the 20th 2031, Tuesday. What was going on?

She got up and began pacing around her tiny flat. As she paced, she realized her day bag was gone from its hook next to the front door. She went over to her dresser and rummaged through the top drawer. The blue swimsuit was gone as well. Her running shoes weren't sitting under her bed and her water bottle wasn't in the cabinet. It was as if the day was playing out as it should be, but she wasn't participating. She felt like an actor who had missed her cue to go on stage.

Sam decided she would go to the pool, because it was Tuesday, damn it, and Tuesday meant she should be swimming laps. If she was having some kind of episode, a delusion of repeated days, then she would stick to her weekly schedule. Predictable chaos. She put on her spare swimsuit, green and without any sensors, under her jeans and laced up an older pair of running shoes. The shoes were also dumb, unable to tell her anything. She would have to do without her phone as it too, was also gone. Being without any of her tech made her feel slightly naked, as if she lost a lifelong companion. The lock picking kit was still in her pocket, which Sam found incredibly comforting, a tangible relic from the day before.

She headed out the door and took a different route to the pool, winding her way through a meticulously, manicured park. As she meandered through the grounds, early morning joggers ran around her. The lawn chairs were empty, waiting patiently for park goers to sit and enjoy the scenery. The spring flowers were just opening up to the sun, flashy purples, pinks, and yellows. The lovely scene clashed wildly with the frantic thoughts going through Sam's mind.

At the large, old, stone building Sam could see the chalk scribbles were still on the sidewalk. Walking around the writing she could see very long equations and diagrams of stars, galaxies, black holes. She patted the nose of one of the lion statues guarding the door as she climbed the steps.

Just as she was about to head up the stairs into the building the large doors opened. Ducking behind a fat old oak tree, Sam watched to her utter amazement, as she walked down the stairs. The doppelgänger Sam was fiddling with her phone.

My phone? Our phone? Sam thought wildly. Sam watched herself put in her earbuds. Sam knew she was listening to the news, because that was what she had listen to that morning. Sam's head was beginning to hurt. She thought she might throw up. Other, oblivious Sam walked away. Sam watched her go. She sat still for a few minutes until she no longer felt nauseous before she started walking to the pool building, mostly because she didn't know what else to do. She could hear people swimming in the warm pool. It would be, she guessed, the pair from yesterday morning (this morning again?).

Sam walked tentatively to the doorway of the pool. The pair of Americans were indeed there, both in the water. The woman swam around while the young man clung to the wall, his feet firmly planted on the ladder. She watched them for a few minutes before Virginia noticed her and shouted, "Hey! You comin' in or just gonna watch us?"

Sam shrugged. She had come here to swim and that's what she was going to do. She kicked off her shoes and pulled off her socks and jeans. She stood for a second with her arms crossed before walking to the edge of the pool. She sat with her feet dangling in the water. Virginia swam towards her and smiled. "Hi! I'm Vir-"

Sam cut her off. "Virginia. And your friend is Stokely."

Virginia gave a laugh. "Have we met before? I'm not always the greatest with names and faces."

Sam answered, "I kind of think we met on a roof but I also kind of think I'm going insane so maybe, yes, we've met before but most likely, no, we haven't met. It was a crazy delusion my brain made up." The pair stared at her for a moment.

Sam stood and walked to the far end of the pool. She knew now she was finally going off the metaphorical deep-end, so why not do so physically as well? She jumped in, released the air from her lungs and sank like a stone to the bottom of the pool. Drawing her knees to her chest, she watched the light above her stream through the water. The chlorine stung her eyes and an uncomfortable burning grew in her chest. She began to feel creeping panic, remembering her dream from the day before (that morning?). As her vision began to tunnel she saw a dark figure swim towards her. The shadow reached out a hand, gripped her around the waist, pulling her to the surface of the water. More hands grabbed her under her arms and hoisted her out of the water. She lay on the cold tile for several minutes with her eyes closed, coughing and gasping.

Someone draped something over her, a very large, soft towel perhaps. Voices were chatting overhead, presumably about her.

"First time, I'll bet you. Met us already. That's how she knew our names." The young woman was speaking. She sounded amused.

"Do most people freak out like that?" This was the young man. He had concern in his voice.

"If they don't know what's going on—yeah. Some people are pre-warned for whatever reason. I was like her, too. Worse maybe. I didn't talk for about three weeks."

"But how are you sure? How do you know she's not just crazy?"

There was a pause and a rustling noise. Finally she answered, "Look here. Just the same as mine. Bet I gave it to her. "

Sam opened her eyes and raised herself up onto her elbows. The pair was sitting on the tile floor a few meters away, watching her with trepidation. Virginia had the lock-picking kit in her hand, which had apparently been liberated from Sam's jeans. Sam sat up and said, "Thank you for pulling me out of the water. I think I'm alright now."

Virginia asked, "So, we've met before now?"

Sam shook her head. "We meet today, but later—in the afternoon. You two were on the roof of my work building, looking at the solar arrays. I think I'm doing the same day over again."

Virginia scooted closer to her, a look of wonderment on her face, "You only went a day? Is that right? That's amazing! You're gonna be a sharp shooter, I'll bet. The Annie Oakley of tempusnauts."

"What's a tempusnaut?" Sam asked.

Virginia smiled. "Tempusnaut: time sailor. Someone who travels through time."

"Oh. Who's Annie Oakley?"

"Annie Oakley is a little before your time I guess. She was a performer from over a century ago. Really good at shooting."

"Oh." There was a long pause. "So am I completely crazy? Or did I really travel through time?"

Virginia laughed a bit. "You really did go back in time. Me and Stokes can do it, too. We can go pretty much whenever or wherever we want, within reason. What's your name by the way?"

"Sam. Nice to meet you again." There was an awkward pause, "So, what now?"

Virginia shrugged. "So what, what now?"

"So what does that mean? What do I do now?"

Virginia answered back, "Do whatever the hell you want to do. You can go exploring on your own, or if you want, you can come with us. Or don't go anywhere, stay right here and now and live a boring normal life."

Sam got to her feet, as did Virginia. The two looked at each other for a minute before Sam said, "I could stay right here?"

Virginia nodded.

"And not go anywhere? And be normal?"

She nodded again. "You might accidentally travel again, especially if you don't practice. It's part of your physiology, like a muscle. If you don't use it a lot you lose control over it."

"Or I could, what? Go to the future and never see my family again?"

Virginia shook her head. "Of course not. You could always come back. Kind of like living abroad for a semester."

"It would be pretty hard to go back to normal life, don't you think?"

"Well of course it would be hard to fit in again but it's not impossible. I've gone to see my family a few times and they never noticed anything off about me. Or anything more off than normal."

Stokely looked at her with genuine surprise on his face. "You've been home? But you said you didn't do that."

Virginia shook her head. "No, I said I wasn't one of those people who went traveling one day and had a normal life the next. But yeah, I've been home, just a few times."

For some reason Stokely looked a bit miffed by this insight. Virginia picked up the cloth that had formerly been draped over Sam. She spoke as she stuffed the cloth into her backpack. "Well it was nice to meet you, but it would appear that according to you, me and my friend must go."

Sam looked at her in confusion, "Go? I never told you to go."

Virginia put her backpack on and handed the lock-picking kit to Sam. "Not specifically. But you did say you met us on a roof sometime today right? So we are going to go say hello."

"Oh. I guess that makes sense. It was on the City of Bath college campus, the roof of the performing arts building. I guess you'll need this kit to get the door open, it's normally locked."

Virginia pulled off her backpack and rummaged in it a bit, pulling out a small leather case that was identical to the one already in Sam's hand.

"Don't need it. I've still got mine."

Sam took the other case from Virginia to compare the two. "Wow, they really are the same. I guess that's a sign that I might not be crazy after all."

Virginia took her case back. "Why do you think you are going crazy?"

Sam squeezed the other case tightly in her fist and gave a halfhearted shrug. "My dad's schizophrenic. He killed himself when I was four. I've always been kinda worried I would end up like him."

The three of them stood in silence for a minute. Sam wasn't sure why she had told the strangers this tidbit of information. Normally, she never talked about her biological father with anyone, even her mother.

Stokely looked at the floor, obviously unsure how to respond. Virginia on the other hand studied Sam with a very particular look.

"That's very unlikely," Virginia said. It wasn't the first time Sam had heard that. Although such a response usually came from one of the many therapists she had seen as an adolescent.

"I know that."

"No, I mean really unlikely. Your dad had an unlucky brain chemistry that he has no control over and it makes you mad or sad or whatever—which is normal. Your risk of having schizophrenia like him is only six percent higher than the normal population, which are pretty good odds."

Sam liked the way she said it, honest and informative, like a good textbook. "You sound like a doctor."

"I am." This too seemed to surprise Stokely. Sam wondered just how much he knew about her.

"What kind of doctor?"

She began ticking off on her fingers, "Neurosurgeon, Nano-surgeon, Anesthetist, Primary Care with a specialty in space, Cryo-Technician, Neonatal Surgeon, Burn specialist, Field Doctor, and Therapist specializing in A.I. and fundamentally altered humans. Some of those aren't a thing yet. I'm working a few more degrees as well."

Sam shook her head. "No way anyone could have that many degrees. That's insane. It takes years to become a doctor of *one* disciple."

Virginia shrugged. "I'm a lot older than I look. You get bored doing the same job for fifty or sixty years. So I change it up a lot. I'll bet I've done just about every job under the sun."

"Like what?" Sam asked.

She flashed Sam a big toothy grin. "A lady doesn't kiss and tell. And anyway—"

All at once Sam's world went wrong for the second time. The smell of oranges and sawdust filled her nose once again and her lunges hitched. Then came the shove to her chest.

Her bare feet skidded on a gravel rooftop and she fell backwards onto her bum. She was on the roof of her work building in what appeared to be the late afternoon. She stood up and brushed off the seat of her bathing suit. She wished she had put her pants back on. At least it was warm out. The bells at the church began to ring. Sam realized after counting the tolls she had missed herself and Beck by only a minute or two. Someone, herself probably, had locked the combination lock on the other side of the door. Of course. How was she going to get down?

Hunting through the lock picking kit, which was thankfully still in her hand, she found all manner of odd tools she had overlooked before. There was a small plastic piece that fit over her finger. It grew warm and the tip shifted to look like a fingerprint. There was a thin film that had the overlay of an eye printed on it. Sam wondered why Virginia kept the other metal tools when everything else in the case was so much more sophisticated.

Tucked into a side pocket was what looked like a small glass vial, no wider than a chopstick and shorter than her pinky finger. When she picked it up it grew warm in her hand and started to contract, like a snake or worm. It stretched itself towards the door, searching for something. Curious, Sam put the device next to the door and it slithered through the crack. A few seconds later she heard a click and the lock was unlatched. When she turned the handle and opened the door she found Virginia and Stokely standing on the other side, grinning at her. In Virginia's hand was the small device, once again looking like a glass vial. She handed it to Sam, who put it back in the case.

"That case belongs to you. Most of that stuff was bio-locked, on you apparently. It doesn't work for me or anyone else."

Sam looked at the case in confusion. "How did you get it? Why is it locked on me?"

Virginia pointed to Stokely. "He gave it to me. But not him, an older one. The same one who told me I would travel with him. He said he was borrowing it from someone and said that I should return it. He was also the one who suggested that Stokes and I take a trip here, to this time. Man, I love when stuff like this happens."

Sam stared at the soft leather case in her hands. She thought of the pictures of presumably herself dancing in France. They felt like postcards from a friend inviting her somewhere or somewhen else. Come find me, your future self. I am a lockpicker, a dancer on stage, an adventurer. She looked at the pair in front of her.

"So if you gave the lock picking kit to Virginia," she gestured to Stokely. "how did you get it in the first place?"

Stokely shrugged. "I don't know. I haven't done it yet. I'll let you know as soon as I do."

Sam bit her lip, thinking. "Do you think maybe, we're friends in the future?"

Virginia smiled brightly at her. "Maybe we travel together sometimes. Seems like future Stokes gave me the kit on purpose, knew you would want it now. Seems like something friends would do, don'cha think?"

"Where are you two going to travel next? "

They both shrugged at the same time.

Stokely said, "Well, we just went to South Dome, a city on the moon. I thought it'd be funny to go back and watch the moon landing when it happens, live on T.V."

"That was in the 60's right?"

He nodded. "1969."

It was like she had left breadcrumbs for herself. "Well, it played on T.V.s all over the world right? Could I come with you? And, um…could we maybe go to France to watch it?"

Virginia clapped her hands like a delighted child. "I love France! I've got a house we could stay at too! And you two could meet some other tempusnauts while we are there, there's loads in Paris at that time."

Stokely smiled. "Viva le Franco. Or something. I don't speak French."

Virginia smiled as well. "That don't matter! I've got a translator in my head. I can speak any language out there." She grabbed his hands and started dancing a silly jig with him and singing in slightly off key French. "Allez, viens boire un pti coup à la maison! Hippa! Ya du blanc, y'a du rouge, du saucisson!"

The two of them fell laughing onto the roof. Sam joined them. Virginia swung her arms around both of their shoulders. "Well it looks like for the time being we are the three time traveling amigos."

Sam, surprisingly, liked the sound of that.

Chapter 4 – Daily Life

Stokely, Sam, and Virginia's first home together was a beautiful townhouse in the La Butte aux Cailles neighborhood of Paris that sat on a narrow, winding street. A sunshine-yellow building, with old paint peeling on the outside was a hidden modern treasure. There were three bedrooms, one for each of them. Strangely, the rooms were already furnished for Sam and Stokely, with clothes that fit perfectly and pictures of their families sat on the bedside tables. Everything had a slightly lived-in feel, as though the original inhabitants of the house had stepped out for a moment and then never returned. Groceries filled the kitchen cabinets, a half-finished puzzle languished on the living room coffee table, and pictures of the three of them decorated the walls, adventures they had yet to experience. A strange looking red and black cat, with a nametag that read Delphi, lived there as well. She followed Stokely everywhere.

When Sam and Stokely asked Virginia about the bedrooms and the pictures she said, "I guess you've lived here before. I haven't bought the house yet; I just gave myself the keys a couple of weeks ago, before I met Stokes. Could be one of you two bought the place for all I know."

They found Virginia usually answered questions in this manner, twisting her words to avoid saying anything concrete about their future or her past. They had no idea where or when she was from.

The house came equipped with far-flung technologies that definitely did not belong in 1969. The oven could take voice commands and a small autonomous vacuum cleaner that could climb stairs buzzed around. Numerous antiques and relics from different time periods littered the house, strewn around carelessly; there was a torn and stained French army uniform mounted on the wall in a glass case, a Stradivarius violin, a small silver makeup case engraved with mother of pearl that Virginia claimed had belonged to royalty.

During their first week in the house Stokely spent most of his time walking around the city, laying in parks and reading books from Virginia's extensive library. He found the future history books particularly fascinating. Virginia encouraged him to read the trivia books, telling him that trivia is the basis of culture and culture is how they would blend in during different time periods. Whenever he hung around the townhouse Delphi remained constantly under foot. She curled up in his lap at the dinner table, pawed his feet playfully when he sat on the couch, and snuggled against his side each night.

Virginia spent most of her time drawing and painting on large canvases set up in the living room and in a plethora of sketchbooks she carted around the city. She also disappeared at times, popping off for a few hours before re-appearing suddenly in the kitchen or the bathtub, her arms filled with gifts from different times and places. She had a detached sort of relationship with objects, not really seeming to realize the worth of anything. One evening, Sam walked into the living room just in time to stop Virginia from painting on a small statue of a woman, which later would be discerned as a Venus figurine predating recorded history. When asked where she got it, Virginia merely shrugged and said it was a gift from a friend. She seemed to have only a very basic grasp of the currency of the time—giving overly large bills to waitresses and telling them to keep the change—much to their astonishment. She would also ask how many euros something cost despite the fact that the euro wouldn't exist for another 30 years.

Sam's spent her days learning the lay of Paris. She went for runs through the different neighborhoods, especially in the evenings, which worried Stokely. She visited several dance schools, searching for the teacher from the photos. No one at any of the places she visited had ever heard of a Madam Curie. It frustrated her, the teasing pictures of a future that wasn't hers just yet.

One evening, after another fruitless day of searching for a woman who didn't seem to exist, Sam stomped into the living room and plopped down on the couch in a huff. When Virginia asked her what was wrong, Sam answered annoyed, "We've been here a week and I haven't found where I'm supposed to dance!"

Sam glared at Virginia, who painted busily by the front window. Virginia paused, her brush hovering in the air. "A week is nothing for us. Do you have a different hairstyle in the pictures of yourself you found?"

The questions confused Sam. "No, it's the same."

"Did you study it very carefully for any new features on yourself, scars or tattoos or piercings? Or signs of aging?"

Sam scowled at her. "No, why would I do that?"

Virginia set her brush down and gave Sam a very pointed look. "You have no way of knowing how old you were in those pictures. How much time must pass for you before it becomes a reality. Patience might be a virtue for regular people but with time travelers it becomes a necessary personality trait. I find it best to simply ignore those little breadcrumbs we get from our future selves unless it is very important or we are giving explicit instructions on what to do. You haven't met your older self yet, haven't come back to tell you where to go, so obviously it will work itself out in time."

It wasn't the advice she wanted to hear, but Sam had to admit she made a good point. Virginia picked up her brush and dipped it in some purple paint. On the marble windowsill she wrote Patience of Self in lovely cursive writing. Sam smiled at her and took the brush. In her own messy spiky handwriting she added Patience in Time.

Sam sighed. "Well, what should I do with my time?"

Virginia offered her a shrug. "Find an activity you like doing and do that for now."

Stokely walked into the room just then, his arms full of mail and paper grocery bags. He sang to himself softly, Sam figured some old band her grandparents probably listened to. He may have looked around the same age as her but his music and fashion came from a noticeably older time. Sam found it funny, the way he always wore what she would consider nice occasion clothes and had trouble with simple technologies, like digital music players.

"What are you girls up to?" he asked on his way to the kitchen.

Sam followed him. "Painting and talking. Virginia was telling me to be more patient."

"Still haven't found your dance school, huh?" Stokely seemed to have a way of always getting straight to a problem.

"No. I don't like this anticipation. I just want to go out and do it." Stokely began putting the groceries away while Sam leafed through the mail. Mostly it was addressed to Virginia, except for the last letter, a heavy purple envelope. It read To VA, Stokes, Samantha. Someone must have slipped it in the mailbox as there was no address or stamp. Sam called Virginia into the kitchen.

"What's up?" Virginia asked. She had smeared yellow and red paint on her cheek.

Sam held up the envelope. "It's for all of us."

Virginia smiled. "Well don't wait, open it."

Tearing open the envelope Sam found a thick card inside which she read to the others.

"Hello little bird, hope you are
well. There will be a party on May 1st
at 6p.m. The usual place in Seizieme

Neuilly. Looking forward to meeting your new travel companions. Love."

Virginia and Stokely crowded next to Sam to see the card. Stokely asked, "Who's it from?"

Sam ran her fingers over the lettering and shrugged.

Virginia grinned broadly. "It's from my friend Adja. Little bird is her nickname for me. There are sometimes these parties for time travelers at her mansion in the Seizieme Neuilly neighborhood. It's really fun, I promise. This is one breadcrumb we should follow."

Sam and Stokely looked at each other. They'd been discussing, between the two of them, the prospect of meeting other time travelers but both felt a little leery. Sam spoke up.

"So, how many other time travelers are there?"

Virginia shrugged, "Dunno. Not very many. A mathematician friend of mine says he guesses out of all the humans ever alive there are probably no more than one thousand travelers. Another friend, he's a professor in the future who studies time travel, he says it's closer to six hundred. Other people think it was more, like about a million or so."

"Wow. That's not a lot."

She nodded. "Yeah, it's really hard to figure out. Time and space are big. Like, really impossibly big. So you could be alive for a long time and never meet another traveler. I didn't meet another one 'til I'd been bumming around for a few years."

It was one of those rare bits of information Virginia gave about herself. Stokely spoke up, hoping to pry more history out of her.

"How did you find other time travelers?"

"Well, they came to me. The first one I met, I don't know how he found me. The next few had already met me and older me told them when and where I first met them."

"Kinda like how we met?"

"Yeah. I think that's the most common way. It's really unlikely for two random time travelers to bump into each other, considering the vastness of time and the sheer number of people who have existed. I'm really glad we found each other; I was alone for a long time. I thought I was going to be on my own forever, just drifting through space. But I didn't want to go back to my time. I never belonged there. And pretty much all the time travelers I do know already have their own companions, their own confidants to travel with."

Sam asked, "But what about your friend who's having the party?"

"Adja? I lived with her for a while. But sharing a home with her is…strange. She's old, older than anyone else, I think. She can travel huge chunks of time, more than anyone else I've ever met. Sometimes she would walk in the door and just stare at me. Like she wasn't sure I was real. She'd touch my face or hug me, smell my hair. The kind of thing family does to you when they haven't seen you in a decade. And after a while, I realized. She hadn't seen me. For decades, centuries. She'd leave in the morning for coffee with a friend and that evening she would be a totally different person. People change over time, but it's gradual. Living with her is like skipping to the end of a book, then going back to chapter two."

"That's kind of how it feels with you sometimes."

She laughed. "You haven't been with me that long yet. But I'm sorry for that. I'll try to be consistent with you. I'm glad we met more normally. With Adja, one day after I'd been living with her for a few years, she asked who I was. It was a younger version of her; she'd never seen me before. I had to explain why I was living in her house. But she wasn't bugged out or anything, because that's a normal day for her, I'm sure."

This was the most information about herself Virginia had ever given Sam and Stokely. For just a few minutes her weird, silly personality was gone. Her guarded self exposed, showing her companions what she really was: a lonely person.

Sam put her arm around Virginia and asked, "So, what kind of party will this be?"

Virginia smiled and said, "The fun kind."

Sam smiled back. "I'm in. Stokes, what about you?"

Stokely nodded. "Sure. Why not?"

Chapter 5 Party

In the week before the party, Virginia took the other two shopping for something to wear. She led them to outrageously priced shops filled with beautiful handmade items. At first, Stokely and Sam balked at the idea of her buying them such expensive clothing. Some of the outfits cost more than a car. They relented eventually, after Virginia threatened to go to the party naked if they wouldn't let her get them something new. Neither of them was sure if she was joking.

Sam picked out a long, dusty gold gown that draped over her slender body. Virginia chose a deep purple dress that hugged her curvy figure. Stokely let the girls decide his outfit for him. Together they chose a white collared shirt with slacks, a vest and a top hat, which were all black. The vest collar was a shockingly bright red that matched a band around the top hat. Stokely thought the bright color looked silly and said as much, but the girls insisted it went wonderfully with his dark skin.

On the night of the party, Virginia walked in on Stokely calling a taxi. She made a face. "I thought we were going to walk."

He laughed. "It's raining. These clothes cost more than a paycheck."

"I guess you have a point."

"What's wrong?"

She shook her head. "Nothing. I just don't like cars. Where's Sam?"

"I think she's still getting ready. You want me to go check on her?" But before she could answer Sam appeared in the doorway. Both Virginia and Stokely stood staring at her for a minute, mouths slightly open.

She looked beautiful. The dress flowed around her tall, slender frame, making her look a bit like a statue. She wore makeup for a change and had clipped a string of pearls to her short curly hair. Around her neck gleamed a slender gold chain with a green stone.

Stokely whistled at her. "Wow. I didn't know you could look like a girl."

She punched him lightly on the arm. "I do girly things sometimes. I can even walk in high heels."

Virginia laughed. "That's better than me. Man you are goin' 'ta get some kind of attention tonight. Just don't let some pretty French boy steal you away from us, ok?"

She blushed a bit, not used to all the flattery.

From outside, a horn beeped. The taxi had arrived. Before leaving, Sam insisted Virginia put on shoes. Her habit of running around barefoot, even in the city, made Sam embarrassed.

They made a mad dash to the taxi, trying to avoid the puddles. Virginia gave instructions to the cab driver and after a few minutes of driving she leaned her head against the fogged up window and shut her eyes. She didn't talk for most of the ride, strange for someone who was normally a chatterbox. After a while, Sam leaned over towards her and asked, "Are you alright?"

She wordlessly shook her head without opening her eyes.

"What's wrong with you?" Stokely asked from the front passenger seat.

"Carsick."

As soon as the taxi pulled up in front of an intimidatingly large mansion Virginia stuffed several bills in the cabby's hand and bolted from the vehicle, not bothering with the umbrellas they had brought. The other two walked a bit slower up the long driveway, picking their way around puddles. Virginia still looked a little green around the gills when they caught up to her at the entranceway of the house.

"You know, Virginia," Stokely mused, "I think you're supposed to get sick after the party is over."

"Well, you know me. I'm prone to doing things out of order."

They rang the doorbell and heard a chime in the house mingled with the sound of party-goers. A tall, imposing redheaded man threw open the large oak doors. He towered over the three of them, all muscle. His face split into a wide toothy grin and he said in a thick, almost impossible to understand Scottish accent, "V! Ah man, long time no see! Come in, come in!"

He moved his large frame out of the doorway to let them pass. They entered into a marble-floored indoor courtyard filled with large potted plants and huge stones set around a fountain. Stokely and Sam openly gawked at the lavish interior of the house.

"This is Stokely and Sam. Seems I've finally got myself some travel companions. Sam, Stokely, this is Hunter Preantepenultimate Pilchard. He's an old friend of mine."

71

Hunter bear-hugged her, lifting her off the ground with ease. He led them to a basement door from which issued sounds of people talking and music. Virginia waved them on. "You guys go on ahead. I'll be down in a second."

As they walked down the long staircase Sam said, "I wonder why Virginia doesn't like riding in cars?"

Stokely shook his head. "That was weird. We went in a spaceship together and she was fine."

This made Hunter laugh. "Spaceships are a lot different than the crazy, unsafe, death machines being driven around now."

He opened a door at the bottom of the staircase with a large sign that read The Dark Room. It led to a large, dimly lit room filled with about a dozen people who were all from different time periods. An Asian woman in a Victorian era dress was dancing with two men in skin-tight bodysuits that lit up, a dreadlocked monk in brown robes stood chatting with a few punk-rock teens decked out in leather and studs. In the corner of the room, a bearded man in a kimono sat on the floor playing a chess game with a tiny, dark skinned, white-haired girl wearing a lab coat. Loud swing music reverberated over the wooden floor. In the middle of the space towered a huge, pillowy fake castle, with four mock towers and mesh screen instead of walls. It was similar to a trampoline, two people jumped around inside, squealing with laughter.

When Stokely asked what the strange structure was Sam said, "A bouncy castle, duh." As if that explained it.

Hunter led them towards a dimly lit bar at the back of the room, the only source of light.

"What do you guys want to drink? They've got this place stocked to the three by three."

They stood in front of the solid mahogany bar. The bartender, a grizzled man with a scar running across his face from ear to ear, smiled at them. When he asked what they wanted Stokely could see a silver metal tongue flash behind his teeth.

The man laughed when Sam rather quietly said, "Anchor Steam?"

Hunter spoke up. "I think they're kinda new Danny. How about two nightlights with cranberry juice? Not too strong."

While the barkeep mixed their drinks, a beautiful, tattoo-covered, blonde woman wearing what appeared to be a dress made out of snakeskin walked over to them and pecked Hunter on the cheek. He wrapped his arms around her waist. "This is my wife, Civic-Lee. Lee, this is Stokely and Sam. They've been traveling with V."

She gave them a warm, friendly smile and said in a purring French accent. "Oh, that's wonderful. I'm so glad to hear she finally has some travel friends."

Danny sat their drinks on the bar and tipped his hat at them. Sam began drinking hers immediately but Stokely eyed it with some suspicion. "What's in this?"

Hunter chuckled. "It's got firefly whisky, spiral sours, and cranberry juice. It'll let you see in the dark. Don't worry it only lasts a few hours."

Sam clinked her glass against Stokely's. "It's really tasty. Try it."

He cautiously took a sip. She was right, it tasted of cranberries, tart and delicious. A delightful tingle lingered on his tongue after he swallowed the chilled liquid. Stokely's eyes quickly adjusted to the gloom as he drank. Hunter led them to a corner of the room where several cushions sat around a low table covered with bowls of snacks.

Stokely sank down on a cushion, absolutely mesmerized by his newfound night vision. He could see everything in the room in perfect detail, despite the low light.

Civic-Lee sat down next to him and grabbed an electric blue drink in a tall skinny glass. She closed her eyes as she sipped it.

"What are you drinking?" Sam asked.

"It's called the Batman chaser. It gives you echolocation, just like a bat. It's a lot of fun. I'm going in the bounce house if anyone wants to join me." As she strolled away her dress rippled and contracted, changing into a bodysuit. Sam pulled off her shoes and ran after her. The pair climbed into the bounce house with shrieks of laughter.

"How long have you known Virginia?" Stokely asked, as Hunter sat down next to him.

Hunter took a sip of his own drink, a green swirling liquid in a wine glass. "Since I was a kid. My parents are travelers, whole family is. I've met you before. You stayed with us for a while when I was a kid. Hang on a sec'."

He held up his right arm, almost completely covered in tattoos. To Stokely's surprise the artwork shifted into a keyboard arrangement. Tapping his fingers against his skin brought up a floating screen. He grinned at Stokely's stunned expression.

"Never seen tech like this before? When are you from?"

Stokely reached out his fingers to touch the screen, but they passed right through it. "I came from the 60's, so now I guess. How are you doing that?"

"It's a holograph screen. There's a computer in the arm. Well the computer is the arm, it's fake."

The screen brought up several pictures of different children. Hunter flipped through them, swiping his hand in the air. He stopped at one of three kids and Stokely. They stood next to the ocean.

"That's amazing. Are those your siblings?"

Hunter smiled. "Yes, there are ten of us kids in the family. You never told me you were from the 60's. Kinda explains your music tastes. You want some snacks?"

He offered up one of the bowls from the table. Peeking inside, Stokely saw it contained crickets. "Umm. No thanks. I'm not hungry."

Hunter laughed as he grabbed a handful and shoved them in his mouth. "I was mostly joking. You wouldn't eat them when I was a kid either. It's the same as meat, just crunchier."

"What happened to your arm?"

He held his arm aloft and pulled back a section of skin on the forearm. The exposed area revealed a metal and plastic interior. "I time traveled while I was drunk. Not normal-happy-buzzed drunk, blackout can't-remember-what-you-did-the-night-before drunk. Materialized with my arm in the ground. Ripped it clean off."

"What do you mean materialized with your arm in the ground?"

"You've never heard of that? Man, you really haven't been doing this long. Ok, so you know how when you close your eyes you can still touch your nose with your hand? You know where your body is in space. Time traveling is tied to that. If your judgment of that is messed with, alcohol or weed or something, you can materialize somewhere wrong. It's a good way to get yourself killed—appear half in one room, half in another, with a wall between. I got lucky."

"Virginia never told me about that."

Hunter shrugged. "She's never been the talking type. You weren't really, either."

"She's plenty talkative, she just doesn't really say anything."

"Ask her to teach you. She's pretty old. The older someone gets, the more they forget how it was to start out at this crazy way of living."

Stokely contemplated this while he finished his drink. The girls came back from the bounce house laughing with flushed cheeks. A skinny, dark-skinned Asian man walked through the crowded room toward Sam and Stokely's small group. He had a coy, handsome face with darker hair and eyes. He settled himself onto a cushion and smiled at Sam.

"Sam, Stokely, this is my brother Sagitta Penultimate Pilchard," Hunter said. "Sagitta, you remember Virginia's travel companions. They've only just met us."

Sagitta took Sam's hand and kissed it lightly. "It's wonderful to see you again. You look stunning."

She blushed and stammered, "Thank you…um…It's nice to meet you."

He nodded towards Stokely. "Everything alright, Stokes? I like your suit."

"Thanks."

Sagitta grabbed a handful of crickets and popped one in his mouth. "We're going swimming in the ocean next week. Want to come? It would be great to catch up with you guys. I haven't seen you since I was a kid."

Sam nodded enthusiastically at the invitation. Stokely however didn't seem as thrilled. "I don't know how to swim."

The two brothers laughed. Hunter said, "You taught me how to swim. You're a great swimmer."

Stokely shook his head. "I never learned. I'm afraid of the water."

Sagitta waved his arm dismissively. "Don't worry about it. We'll teach you how, return the favor. We're going down to the Côte Sauvage."

Sam looked a little concerned. "I've been there, it's beautiful. But isn't the surf too rough for someone who doesn't know how to swim?"

"We know a nice cove where the water is gentle."

Stokely took off his top hat and nervously fidgeted with it in his lap. "I'll go but I don't think I'll go in the water."

The two brothers looked slightly disappointed. Hunter said, "You can hang out with our sister, Cass, in the tide pools. Her kid self's here right now and she doesn't know how to swim very well yet."

Hunter and Sagitta got up and headed to the bouncy house. Civic-Lee placed her hand on Stokely's shoulder. "Don't worry about it. Bring a book or something and you can read on the sand. You don't have to go in the water with them."

Sam stood up and stretched, reaching her long arms towards the ceiling. "I'm going to get another drink. Either of you want something?"

They both shook their heads. Sam walked off, holding her shoes in her hand. She stopped to talk with a man wearing a knight's helmet, a tuxedo, and house slippers. The man pulled off his heavy, metal helmet and stuck it on Sam's head. Stokely heard his friend laughing as she pushed up the visor and turned to wave at him. He waved back. Civic-Lee leaned over and said, "He's really a knight you know, from the fourteen hundreds. Travels hundreds of years in one go, I've heard, or maybe more. Can't imagine what that's like. He's Adja's husband."

Stokely turned to Civic-Lee and said, "I should go check on Virginia. She's been gone a long time."

"Her room is on the second floor. Third door on the right."

Stokely walked out of the dark room and up the stairs. The lights in the main part of the house jarred his eyes. Everywhere he looked he saw halos reflecting off metal and glass. He rubbed his eyes, trying to get rid of the after-images. As he walked towards the large, wood staircase that led to the second floor when he heard a giggle and a small British voice whisper, "Stokes. Watch out. There are pirates."

Peering around, he spotted a small smiling face looking out at him from under the huge dining room table. Blankets covered the table to create a fort. The child, a tiny, freckle-faced Indian girl, crawled out from under the table. She held in her hand what Stokely hoped was a toy gun. She pointed it to Stokely's left and pulled the trigger. A glowing man in pirate garb appeared and exclaimed, "Argg. Where be the treasure?"

Stokely jumped and fell over, startled by the man's sudden appearance. The pirate disappeared and the little girl dissolved into a pile of giggles. When she stopped laughing she tiptoed quietly over to where Stokely sat on the floor, his heart still thumping wildly. She examined his face and said, "You've got cats eyes. I'm not allowed to have cat eyes yet. Did I scare you?"

He nodded. "Yep. I think my heart stopped."

The little girl placed her tiny hand on his chest. "It's still beating. You're exasperating. Mama says that when I say something that's not true but not really a lie."

The girl pulled the trigger on her gun again and the pirate appeared as before. This time he yelled, "X marks the spot!" before disappearing.

It was, Stokely realized, a very sophisticated children's toy. He felt silly for not grasping that immediately.

"I think you mean exaggerating. Exasperating is how you make her feel when you exaggerate."

The little girl placed her hands on her hips and said, "You didn't give me a hug. Are you mad at me?"

Her overly serious expression made Stokely laugh. "No, definitely not. I don't normally hug people I've never met before."

Her eyes got wide. "Oh! This is your first time meeting me! Well ok." She smoothed her skirt and held out one small hand for Stokely to shake. "Hello. My name is Cass Verso Pilchard. It is very, very extra nice to meet you, Stokely, for your first time."

She was the most self-possessed child Stokely had ever met. He shook her hand. "It's very nice to meet you as well. I think we're going to the ocean together next week."

She clapped her hands delightedly. "There are tide pools! We can look at the little crabs!"

"So I've heard. But right now I want to go check on my friend. She's upstairs, I think."

Cass nodded and gestured towards the staircase with her ray gun. "You mean Virginia, right? She went upstairs a while ago with Ms. Adja. I can show you her room."

Without waiting for an answer, she took Stokely's hand and led him up the staircase. She opened a purple and white door without bothering to knock. Outside, the full moon broke through the rain clouds, filling the room with a thin light. Virginia was nowhere to be seen. Cass ran over to the large window where a telescope was set up. She stood on tiptoe to peer through the eyepiece.

A large queen-sized bed, the old wooden kind with curtains, dominated the room. There was a writing desk and a large dresser in a corner, above which hung an enormous circular mirror. Here and there were little mementos of Virginia, like memories carelessly strewn about. Books were piled on the floor and chair next to the desk. As Stokely browsed the titles Cass said, "You know it's not really full tonight. It's full tomorrow and again at the end of the month. It's going to be a blue moon, only it's not really blue."

He walked to the dresser, a cluttered mess of letters, glass perfume bottles, and jewelry. He picked up a small, engraved silver ring set with a purple stone. When his fingers brushed the stone it lit up and began projecting a small holographic video of people in robes throwing mortarboards into the air. It looped this one small scene over and over, everyone in the video perpetually smiling and cheering. Cass came up quietly behind Stokely and held out her hand.

"Can I see?"

He handed the ring to her and she pinched the stone, the hologram disappeared. She put it on her thumb, but it was much too large. She held out her hand and admired it anyway. "One day, I'll finish school and I'll get one too. Mine's going to have a green stone. Do you have a school ring Stokely?"

He shook his head. "I never finished high school."

"Neither did mama." She handed the ring back to him. He inspected it closely. Along the side it said *Saint Louis Class of 2442*. He set the ring back down and caught his reflection in the mirror. His eyes looked strange in the dim light, the pupils huge and gleaming.

Murmured voices and footsteps rang from the hall. Virginia entered the room, clicking on the light switch. Stokely shielded his sensitive eyes from the harsh brightness. He could hear Cass talking with Virginia and someone else, a soft warm voice with just the hint of an accent he couldn't place. He lowered his arm slowly, blinking back tears. A small black woman watched him out of the corner of her eye. She was one of the most beautiful women he had ever seen, with dark ebony skin and a graceful profile. She offered him a small smile.

Virginia walked over to him and placed her hand on the side of his face. "You have cat eyes. Been having fun at the party?"

He nodded. The woman walked over to them and held out her hand. "My name is Adja. I'm an old friend of Virginia's. It's nice to meet you."

As Stokely shook her hand he couldn't help but think that she too had probably met him before and this was just a polite formality. He said, "It's nice to meet you too. Your house is beautiful."

She dipped her head at the compliment. Her movements were like a piece of silk fluttering in the air. Stokely felt suddenly shy around the beautiful woman, any words he was going to say stuck in his throat. Virginia slipped her hand into his and said, "Should we join the others downstairs?"

Adja nodded and turned to Cass. "Little one, I think it is time for you to be off to bed."

The small child hugged each of them in turn and scampered out of the room.

The music had changed to rock. Birds made of different colors of light flew around the room, occasionally flying through partygoers to squeals of laughter. Sam ran over to the group excitedly. After Virginia introduced her to Adja, Sam said, "You have to come meet this cool guy I just met! He's over at the bar, come on."

A tall, slender man stood by the bar, talking to the bartender. When he turned around Stokely saw Virginia stiffen slightly and Adja's pace slowed by just a half step. The man smiled widely, a row of gleaming white teeth with a few gold caps thrown in. He wore a pinstripe suit and had a brass and wood cane hooked over his arm. He gave a short bow to them.

"Hello, Sam's been telling me all about ya."

His accent was Philadelphian. Virginia eyed him up before saying, "Have we met before?"

He looked bemused as he shook his head. "No, I don't believe so. I think I would remember a face as pretty as your's. Although I suppose you coulda met me and I just haven't had the pleasure yet."

Adja stepped forwards to offer her hand. "Well I haven't had a formal introduction, which is odd considering this is my home. I'm Adja."

He took her hand and kissed it. "Tony Eldridge. Lovely to meet ya. I came with the Sortir twins. I hope that was alright."

Danny spoke up from behind the bar. "Virginia, you want something to drink?"

She nodded and said, "Ginger ale."

Tony laid his hand on the bar top. "You a lightweight there, dame? Danny-boy there's got stronger houch if you be wantin' somethin'."

"I'm fine with this."

Tony smiled again and winked at Sam. He was extremely handsome. Several of the other women in the room were sneaking peeks at him and whispering behind their hands to one another. He spoke, to no one in particular, "This party's just the bee's knees, itn't it? And this music's swell. Nutin' like it in my time. You got some neat kinda doohickies I ain't ever seen before."

He grabbed Sam's hand, spun her in a small circle, and started to dance. She giggled like a delighted child. Stokely could see Sagitta across the room watching them. He looked thoroughly annoyed at the dancing pair, his skinny arms crossed over his chest.

As they danced Sam asked, "Have you not been very far into the future?"

He shook his head. "No, I can't get outa this damn century."

Tony stopped dancing and said to Adja, "Hey doll, mind if I have a ciggy?"

Adja crossed her arms. "Sorry. There is no smoking permitted in my home. You will have to step outside."

As he excused himself and headed up the stairs Sam made a move to follow him, but Virginia held her back and shook her head. "No, sorry kid, not that one."

Sam looked confused. "What's wrong? He's nice."

"He's not good. I know him, or knew him."

"Why's he not good?"

"Trust us," Adja said. "He just isn't."

Virginia grabbed Sam's arm and dragged her towards the dance floor. "Enough talk. Let's dance."

Chapter 6 – Beach Trip

The following week Sam, Stokely, and Virginia headed out early on the train to a small town in the country. From there, they were met by: Hunter, Civic-Lee, Sagitta, and Cass. They rented a large black van for the afternoon. As they drove to the beach the sky started to darken, clouds gathering in the distance. A slight sprinkle of rain began to fall, giving everything a wet sheen.

As they drove through fields of lavender, Sagitta rolled down his window. The pleasant smell of the flowers mixed with a hint of rain flooded the van.

Hunter stretched out his arms as best he could, his overly tall frame uncomfortable after several hours of riding in a cramped car.

"How come we didn't jump there? This is boring," Cass said with a pout. She curled up in the back next to a sleeping Virginia, drawing pictures in the fogged up window next to her seat.

Civic-Lee smiled at her. "It's good to remember how everyone else moves around. Not everyone is as good at traveling as you are, little tempusnaut."

Cass smiled, pleased with the compliment.

They drove along a small country road next to the ocean. Huge rocks and boulders sat in the water, waves crashing fiercely against them. They turned down a long, secluded driveway, stopping at a huge white house nestled between a thicket of trees. Cass and Virginia jumped out of the van as soon as it stopped and ran for the small cove behind the house, not bothering to put on rain jackets in the light drizzle. Hunter followed them at a jog.

Adja waited on the porch, sipping coffee from a mug and looking as lovely as ever. Stokely felt himself blush when she said hello and gave him a small peck on the cheek.

As they carried bags into the house, Civic-Lee turned to Stokely and Sam. "You two started traveling a little while ago, right? Have you figured out your limits yet? What you're better at?"

Stokely said, "I've played around a bit. Virginia usually helps both of us with big chunks of time. Anything over 10 years. I think I'm better through space. I've gotten from Mississippi to London in one jump."

Adja whistled. "That is impressive. How about you, love? "

Sam shrugged. "I dunno. I haven't really tried much yet. We came here, but Virginia was helping me. All the jumps I've done myself were really short, a day or a few hours, never more than a few kilometers from where I started."

Adja smiled. "Sounds as if you will be very precise with practice. People who travel short spans can typically appear within a few minutes or seconds of when they want."

"Have you known a lot of travelers?"

She nodded. "I've known many."

"When did you come from?"

She touched her finger to her cheek, thinking. "A very long time ago. Before there were pyramids in Egypt."

Sam and Stokely gawked at her. This enticed a laugh from Adja.

"I can travel thousands of years at a time. That's my specialty, you could say."

At just that second Virginia strolled into the house, soaking wet and looking like a drowned cat. Sagitta barked a laugh at her and asked, "Did you fall in the ocean?"

"No. I jumped in. It's going to start raining heavily in a few minutes so I figured I'd be proactive."

Sagitta laughed again. He always seemed to be laughing, "Boy we picked a great week to come to the beach."

Virginia consulted one of her watches, a green one in the middle of her arm. "The rain should last for only twenty three minutes. Rest of the week's nice. By Sunday it should be downright hot."

After Adja showed everyone around, Sagitta and Virginia set about making dinner. Everyone else went down to the water's edge. Just as Virginia predicted, the rain quit around six in the evening, the sun slinking low on the horizon but not yet setting. Cass ran around excitedly picking up every shell, bit of seaweed, and stick of wood she found. She and Stokely made a sand castle out of her treasures and wet sand, packing everything together with their hands. Sam took off for a run along the beach promising to be back within the hour. Adja stood with her feet in the water, singing a song in an unrecognizable language.

"What language is that?" Stokely asked as he brushed the sand off his hands and joined her at the ocean's edge.

"Mine. It is a dead language."

Cass splashed through the small waves lapping the shore, soaking her shorts. "You should program my translator to understand it, then we could talk in it, and then it won't be dead!"

"That would be very hard to do, little one. It would be very difficult for a computer to learn. I'm not sure I could."

"That sucks. Maybe you could just teach me it, you know, the hard way like people use to do. I've learned QSL that way."

Adja nodded. "You will learn it eventually."

Stokely suddenly remembered Cass telling him her class ring would have a green stone. He wondered how much of her life she already knew about, how strange it must be to have everything laid out before you like a map. He also wondered why the adults in her life seemed to so freely give her information about her future. Didn't that seem strange to them?

He turned to Adja and asked, "What's QSL?"

"It's the hand sign language on Quintus, a colonized planet from Cass's time. Most of the people who live there are deaf."

"On the whole planet? Why?"

Hunter spoke up. "Unusual part of the planet. It's a world really similar to ours, about the same size as Earth—oxygen atmosphere, located in the system's goldilocks zone. That's the zone where life can exist. It didn't need to be terraformed like most of the planets we colonized. But there's a constant background noise coming from the native plants—or as near to plants as is there. Like a high pitched whine, it makes you go deaf if you live there more than a few years."

"Why live there if it makes you go deaf?"

"Wealth, for a lot of people. Lots to mine, lots of space. Quintus was just getting over an extinction period when humans arrived, so there wasn't a lot of native life to compete with. Mostly just the weird plant stuff and a few small animals, some bugs. And a lot of deaf people moved there when the planet was first being colonized. On Quintus deafness isn't seen as a disability, it's an advantage."

After an hour everyone was called in to dinner. Sam came in after everyone was seated, a few minutes late and flushed from her run. They ate a delicious meal: roasted vegetables with garlic chicken, soft buttery rolls, and several different kinds of cheese. There were also several bottles of fine red wine, which Hunter liberally poured into everyone's glass, including Cass's. When Hunter saw Stokely and Sam's confused expressions he laughed.

"Don't worry," he said as he topped off his own cup. "She just likes the taste. She can't get drunk. Her mods won't let her."

"Mods?" Sam asked.

"Modifications. Nano's mostly, keep her healthy. They've replaced vaccines. Mom programed Cass's mods, all my sisters' and brothers' mods, so they can't or couldn't get drunk 'til they're legally old enough. She kinda freaked out about my arm."

"Your arm?"

Sam hadn't seen it before and Stokely hadn't told her about it. Hunter grinned at her before holding up his heavily tattooed arm. The ink once again shifted into a keyboard configuration.

"Wow. Is there a computer in it?"

Sam immediately perceived the arm to be fake, something Stokely hadn't picked up on until Hunter told him. It made him feel more out of time than normal. Sam, more than him, belonged around these other travelers.

Sam inspected Hunter's arm. "It's so life like. It's got a heartbeat!"

Hunter seemed pleased. "Yeah. It bleeds too, not real blood, but close enough so people won't normally notice. And that's a chameleon skin. If I get tan or my skin changes color it'll match. You've got computer chips in prosthetics from your time, right?"

She nodded. "Yeah."

"Well as computers got better, smaller, they started building prosthetics better so eventually you almost can't tell the difference. And, eventually you can have ones with computers like mine. It's really useful. Except it needs some kind of interface. Some people wear a ring or a bracelet that makes a projected keyboard on any surface, some people even have it set up to be compatible to voice commands. Some people," he inclined his head towards Virginia, "use a wrist watch."

Cass spoke up, "Virginia you have a computer arm too? Can you do stuff with it like Hunter?"

Virginia looked confused. "Yeah I do. Hunter, how did you know about my arm?"

"You came to mom once to have it fixed."

Cass, in the innocent way children ask things adults never would, said, "What happened to your arm?"

Virginia looked down at her left arm, lightly touched it with her right hand. "I had an accident when I was young."

Civic-Lee stood up. "I think I'll go get the dessert. Cass would you like to help me carry it in?"

Cass jumped up, happily running into the kitchen. Sagitta stood as well and followed. "I'll help you two out."

The room quieted after the trio left. Virginia stared at her plate, absentmindedly tapping one of her watch faces. It lit a different color with each tap: yellow, red, purple, blue.

Hunter awkwardly played with his napkin, twisting it around his hand. He looked up. "I'm sorry."

Virginia shook her head. "It's fine."

Sam spoke up, "So, you have a fake arm?"

She nodded.

"How did it happen?"

"Told you. An accident."

"What kind of accident? Car accident?"

Stokely had immediately figured that, considering her strong dislike of cars. But, for some reason that didn't seem plausible to him. He had managed to dodge a bullet by traveling, so wouldn't she be able to disappear out of a car before it crashed?

Virginia shrugged her shoulders and continued to tap on the watch face. Yellow, red, purple, blue.

"Was it the first time you traveled?"

A shake of her head.

"Why don't you want to tell us?"

Tap, tap, tap. Yellow, red, purple. "I...I just don't like to talk about it. I was...it was an accident. I had a head injury," she paused, biting her lip. "And I couldn't see where I was going."

Stokely moved to the chair next to her and put his arm around her shoulders. "I'm sorry."

She leaned her head on his arm. "Why would you be sorry? Not your fault."

"I know. But I can still be sorry it happened. You don't have to tell us about it, but you don't have to be embarrassed about it either, ok?"

"Ok."

The others came back in the room, each carrying plates with homemade brownies and ice cream. Civic-Lee ate a spoonful and said, "Oh my, this is heavenly. Who taught you two to cook?"

Just as Virginia said Sagitta's name, he said hers. They both looked at each other and began to laugh.

Sam spoke up. "You two should start a restaurant together. 'Time Traveler Treats' or something like that."

Virginia grinned. "Mobius Strip Muffins. Temporal Tamales."

Adja chimed in. "Black Hole Black-currant Jam? Super-nova Snacks? Spacey Soufflé?"

Several of them laughed. Hunter said, "I think that last one might have another meaning in some circles."

Cass asked perplexed. "What does it mean?" Which only made everyone laugh more.

Cass looked a bit cross. "What? What does it mean?"

Hunter affectionately mussed her hair. "Don't worry. You'll figure it out eventually."

The conversation drifted to other topics: places they had been, famous people they had met, plans for the week, until gradually, one by one, they drifted off to bed.

****

The next morning, Stokely came downstairs and found Lee making pancakes with Cass in the kitchen. They both wore their bathing suits already. Breakfast was laid out and all the people in the house found their way to the table, drawn by the delicious aromas wafting from the kitchen. After eating, everyone helped clean up before getting ready for the day.

They hauled beach chairs and towels out to the sandy beach. Virginia's weather predictions proved correct, and the day grew steadily warmer, not a cloud in the sky. They all splashed at the edge of the shore or, if they felt a bit braver, swam out to a wooden platform floating in the murky deep water. Hunter and Sagitta tried to get Stokely to learn to swim, but he refused.

"No one has ever gotten me into deep water before and you definitely aren't going to be the first," Stokely shied away from the darker water.

Hunter rolled his eyes. "You taught some of us to swim. So we know eventually you learn. This seems as good a time as any."

But Stokely was resolved not to go. He and Cass built castles for a while and when she grew tired of that, the two of them wandered around the shoreline, looking for interesting shells and crabs. About half a mile down the beach, they found a cluster of small cottages amongst a thicket of trees. For a second, Stokely thought he saw a figure watching him from the shadows of the small grove, but he couldn't be certain. Cass caught a particularly large crab and wanted to show her brothers, so they headed back.

Most of the day was spent at the beach. Virginia went back to the house for a bit before returning with lunch. They ate while lounging on blankets on the sand, and returned to the water after eating. All but Stokely and Virginia.

Stokely lay down on a beach blanket, his eyes closed. "There are a couple of cottages up the beach."

"Hm?" Virginia murmured, her mind on the book she was reading.

"Thought I saw someone watching me and Cass while we were walking."

He could hear her put down her book. "You did?"

He opened his eyes. She had a slightly worried look on her face. "What? Something wrong?" he asked.

She paused before answering. "No, probably not. Hope not. Did you get a look at the person?"

He shook his head.

"Well it's probably nothing to worry about."

The two of them sat quiet for a few minutes. Virginia opened her mouth to say something, but then thought better of it.

"What?" Stokely asked.

"I'm," she paused. "I'm not embarrassed about my arm. I just wanted to tell you that. It doesn't embarrass me. It's just, when I lost it, it was a really bad time. I don't like to talk about it and I know people. People eventually ask what happened. I didn't want to lie about it to you and Sam, so I just didn't say anything."

"You lie to us all the time."

She looked slightly hurt at that. "No I don't. When have I lied to you?"

He shrugged. "We don't really know who you are. I have no idea how old you are. Or where you're from."

She placed her book on the ground and drew her knees to her chin. Sitting with her arms wrapped around her legs, she looked younger to Stokely, like a kid being scolded.

"I didn't lie about my age. I really can't remember what it is. I never kept track. And I just never told you where I'm from. That's not lying, it's an omission. And, Stokely—" She stopped talking, took a deep breath and held it. With her eyes closed she slowly let the air out. "I've never told anyone, except Adja, but I didn't lose my arm in an accident. Well, it was accidental on my part, but the rest of it was intentional. I was attacked by…by someone. And we had a fight, and stuff happened, and I wound up without an arm."

"What happened to the guy who attacked you?"

"I got away from him."

"And?"

"Well, he's a time traveler, too. So, I got away from him, but, you know, he could still find me."

Stokely thought about the implications of that answer for a minute before speaking again. "You're worried. You're worried he'll find out where you're from and hurt your family."

With her head tucked down, she nodded slightly.

"I think that's maybe why I never told myself about you and Sam, even though older me knows how lonely I was. Maybe I'm worried he would find you two and hurt you."

From the water came loud shrieking, laughter. Stokely could see the others swimming out to the floating platform, taking turns leaping into the water.

Stokely asked, "Why don't you just go to your family and check on them? Make sure this guy never finds them and hurts them."

"I'd have to check the whole of their lives, look up how they die. I don't want to do that—don't want to know that."

"Oh. Yeah, I wouldn't want to know that either."

"I'm a little worried, because my father died before I was born and my family was always kinda hazy on the details. I'm worried I caused it. But I don't want to know for sure."

"Did your mom raise you all alone?"

She shook her head. "No. My mother died too. I was raised by my aunt and uncle, they never had kids."

Stokely gave her a funny look.

"What?"

"Me too."

"Me too?"

"I was raised by an aunt and uncle. They had kids though, three of them. My folks died in a car accident when I was five. Car went into a lake. I was the only one who got out."

Virginia looked at him, stricken.

"What?"

"That's horrible, Stokely. I'm so sorry."

He shrugged. "It happened a long time ago. My aunt and uncle were good parents to me."

Virginia stared at the ground, scooping up sand and letting it run through her fingers. "You could go back to your family anytime you want. I know people who've done it. One of the Pilchard's, a man named Chamaeleon, gave up traveling all together. He's married, has a normal family. Just say the word and I'll bring you back."

He thought about this. "I don't want to go back, at least not right now. But I do want you to teach me more about traveling. You haven't really shown me or Sam anything."

She nodded. "Ok."

Sam ran up on the beach just then. She shook out her hair over Stokely, sprinkling icy water on him.

Virginia laughed. "Your ears must be burning. We were just talking about you."

"Only good things, I hope." She sat down next to Stokely, wrapping a towel around her shoulders.

Stokely lay back down on the sand. "I wrangled a promise out of her to teach us more about traveling."

Sam gave him a huge grin. "When can we start?"

Virginia raised an eyebrow at her. "I didn't realize you two were so eager to have me teach you. I'm probably not that great a teacher, just warning you now. How about we wait 'til this trip is over? We'll go somewhere in the countryside."

It sounded good to them. The day was almost spent, the sun beginning to dip towards the horizon. When the golden orb disappeared and the twinkling stars came out, they built a fire on the beach. They ate hot dogs and roasted marshmallows and sang songs until everyone felt sleepy. Hunter carried a sleeping Cass back to the house.

Not a single one of them had noticed the man watching them during their merriment. Nor did they see him watch them make their way back to their home, a cigarette clamped between his lips, the flared tip occasionally lighting up his face.

Chapter 7 - Fight

On the third day at the beach, Stokely awoke to the sound of unfamiliar music. When he made his way down to living room he found Sam and Cass dancing together. Sam held the little girl in her arms and they slowly turned in circles around the room. They sang along with the scratchy voice that issued from the music player. After a minute, Stokely recognized the song as a strange version of an old Lead Belly diddy.

"My girl, my girl, don't lie to me. Tell me where did you sleep last night."

When the song finished, Sam smiled at him and said, "Good morning, gramps."

"Gramps?" he asked, with a look of confusion. Technically she was older than him.

She giggled as she put Cass down. "Your clothes. They always look like something my granddad would wear."

Stokely looked down at his outfit, a simple collared shirt and a pair of slacks. "What else would I wear?"

She shrugged. "I dunno. It's just weird to see you dressed like you're going to a job interview or something. We're at the beach."

He shook his head. "We're in my time, remember? Really, you're the one who looks strange." She wore a pair of jean shorts and a purple one-piece bathing suit. At night, the white stripes on the suit lit up, throwing a soft glow over everything near her.

They were more or less on their own for breakfast. According to a note on the kitchen counter, Lee, Sagitta, Hunter, and Adja had gone out on a boat in the early morning and Virginia was out swimming. Sam made the three of them eggs in a basket, her specialty. While they tidied the dishes, they heard shouting from outside and headed to the front door to investigate, Cass running ahead. She grabbed the doorknob, just about to turn it, when a sharp, echoing pop rang through the house. She looked back at Sam and Stokely with large eyes.

Stokely pulled her away from the door and kneeled down to her height. "Listen to me, Cass. I want you to go back in the kitchen, hide in the pantry, alright? If you hear that noise again go back to your time immediately."

Her lip quivered as she nodded at him. She turned and dashed back to the kitchen. Sam looked at him, fear evident in her face.

"What was that noise, Stokely?"

"Gunshot."

They stared at each other for a half second, the color draining out of Sam's face. Stokely took a deep breath before putting his hand on the door handle. He opened the door a crack, peering out. Everything looked normal, the hammock on the porch gently swaying in the breeze, the sound of the waves crashing against the shore. The two of them quietly crept out of the house.

Stokely pushed Sam behind him and whispered, "Keep your head down. If I say go, I want you to jump, ok? Just try to go an hour or two."

"Boy, I sure wish Virginia had given us those time travel lessons a while ago," Sam hissed in his ear. He shushed her. Stokely tried to decide which direction the shot had come from, toward the beach or the road, when someone shouted at them from the water.

"Hey! I know you're out here! You had best get over here or this gal's gonna be in a world of hurt!"

When they reached the shore they saw Tony Eldridge, the man from the party. Virginia lay on the ground, her back to them. Tony held a gun in one hand, which he waved in their general direction. His other hand, at his side, wrapped taut around Virginia's long hair, her head pulled several inches off the sand. Stokely couldn't tell if she was breathing.

Tony grinned at them, several gold teeth flashing in the bright sun. "Well hello there, pretty little lady. I've been wanting to see you again, but your friend here didn't seem to think that was a good idea. She tried to dissuade me."

He let go of her hair, letting her head drop to the ground. He pushed her onto her back with his foot so they could get a good look at her. He'd shot her in the face, taking off most of her jaw. Her eyes wide open, staring at Sam and Stokely. She took a choking gasping breath through her ruined mouth.

Sam made to take a step towards her but Stokely held her back. He called out to Tony, "What do you want?"

He pointed his finger at Sam. "Her."

Stokely pulled Sam towards him and whispered, "Go. Now."

Before either of them could move, however Tony pressed a button on the side of his gun. A flash of pain ran up Stokely's body accompanied by the smell of burning flesh. Momentarily the world turned off, everything going black.

When he came to, he was lying on the ground. Tony held up an unconscious Sam his arm around her waist. Her head lolled to one side. He turned his gun towards Stokely, the barrel level with his head. Stokely could feel himself began to lose his grip on this time, his ears ringing and his head spinning. As light began playing across his field of vision he knew, for the first time, when he was going. He felt it like the first time he learned to ride a bike, when he found that balance point and told himself he would never lose it. He knew with absolute certainty his body, because of fear or stress or panic, was pulling him three weeks into the future and seven miles west. And as Tony pulled the trigger on his gun Stokely did something he had never done before.

He told himself no.

He told himself he would not go randomly into time and space. He would not allow his panicked mind to throw him chaotically to a far-flung destination. Instead, he focused on a spot on the beach, a short walk away in front of a cluster of houses. The place he had been to the day before with Cass. He saw it in his mind's eye.

Not through time, only space. Not through time, only space. He repeated these words over and over in his head as the scene around him dissolved. Suddenly he was there. The clearing of trees stood in front of him, the small houses looking quiet and undisturbed by his sudden appearance. He shakily stood up, the sand scorching. Upon closer inspection he saw burns, going from his feet to mid torso.

He hurriedly made his way back towards the beach house, praying he had stayed at the right time. The sun didn't seem any different and the temperature in the air felt the same. After a few minutes of running, he came up to their small chunk of beach. A large boulder blocked his view but just as he was about to round it, he heard a gunshot.

Tony called out a single angry, "Fuck!" before there was a popping sound, like a champagne cork.

He peered around the rock and felt his heart sink. Tony was gone and he had taken Sam with him. Stokely ran over to Virginia, who lay on the ground, still trying to suck in wet, gasping breaths. It sounded like she was choking on her own blood. As gently as possible he picked her up and carried her back to the house. She felt light in his arms, her warm blood seeping into his shirt. She jerked one arm up and her glazed eyes rolled up to look at him.

"Virginia, lay still. We're almost back to the house. Please, stop moving."

It took all his concentration to stay focused. He knew he couldn't panic just yet. He needed to get his friend back to the house. He needed to get help, needed to find Sam. He really needed the searing pain in his legs to stop.

As he made his way up the stairs the front door opened for him. Cass stood there, eyes wide. She held a large white box in her hands.

"I thought I told you to go back to your time."

She shook her head. "You need the first aid kit."

He pushed past her into the house. He turned to take Virginia into the living room when Cass tugged on his arm.

"Come on, in the kitchen."

She must have seen them walking to the house. The kitchen table had been cleared, the chairs pushed along the far wall to make room. Stokely carefully laid Virginia down. Her breathing didn't sound as loud now. He wondered if that was because it was stopping altogether.

"Where's Sam?"

"Gone. Taken."

She looked at him quietly for a second, her lip quivering and a hint of tears starting up, before placing the first aid kit down on the floor.

Stokely was about to rub his face with his hands when he realized blood covered them and stopped himself. "Hey, Cass? Do you know if any of the others have one of those…those phones that don't plug into the wall?"

She stared at him a moment. "A cell phone?"

He nodded.

She tapped her ear twice with her finger and started talking, but not to Stokely. "Ms. Adja? We need help, Virginia's hurt real bad and Stokely's hurt too and he says Sam's gone."

A snapping noise filled the kitchen and Adja appeared in the room. A second later, two Civic-Lees materialized, each with her arms around either Sagitta or Hunter. The Lee holding Sagitta dropped her arms and disappeared. Hunter picked up Cass and took her out of the room.

Adja approached the table, tenderly placing a hand on Virginia's forehead. "Oh, little bird."

Stokely spoke up from the floor. "It was that guy, Tony. He was at your party. He wanted Sam, he took her."

To Stokely's muddled mind it seemed as if Adja had a look of relief on her face, almost like it was good news. She nodded. "That we can deal with."

Sagitta grabbed the first aid box and began rummaging through it. He pulled out a sheet of grey stickers, peeled one off, and stuck it on Virginia, just below her collarbone. He turned to Stokely and said, "That'll let her sleep."

More things were pulled out of the first aid kit. Adja sprayed a fine, white mesh over Virginia's jaw that grew to cover the whole wound. Sagitta gave her a shot from a syringe filled with a dark red, syrupy liquid. Lee crouched next to Stokely, placing her hand on his shoulder. "She's going to be fine. I know it looks bad, but these sorts of injuries aren't the same to her as they are to you. Now I need to fix those burns, alright?"

Stokely had forgotten about the injury. He said in a slow, slurred voice, "It doesn't hurt that much. It's alright."

Lee shook her head. "You're going into shock. Just sit still, alright?"

She sprayed the white mesh all over his burns. It brought back the feeling. A wave of pain washed over Stokely and he jerked away from her violently.

"Sorry, it's fixing the nerve damage. It's going to hurt. Just, please, be still. Sagitta?"

She looked to her brother-in-law. He hurried over to them, the sheet of sleeping stickers in his hand. Stokely pulled away from them, trying to stand. "No, I need to find Sam. He's going to hurt her."

His knees buckled as soon as he stood up. Sagitta caught him and sat him back down on the floor. "We'll find her, Stokes. We won't let anything happen to her."

Before Stokely could protest further, he felt the cool sticker pressed against his skin. The world started fading, his vision going fuzzy. He could hear people talking, feel hands touching his neck, and then he was asleep.

Sometime later, Stokely groggily opened his eyes. He was on the couch in the living room. Dim evening light from the setting sun diffused through the drawn gauzy curtains, and filled the room. Someone had washed the blood off him and changed his clothes. He got up, letting the blanket that covered him fall to the floor. His legs felt tingly and sore, but otherwise all right. He turned to see Adja sitting on the loveseat, watching him quietly, her dark eyes giving away no hint of her emotions.

"How are you feeling?" she asked.

"Alright. How's Virginia? Is she ok?"

Adja nodded. "She is fine. You were out longer than her. Those electrical burns were very bad. We had to repair your heart's rhythm."

Loud footsteps thumped down the stairs and Virginia appeared in the doorway, sliding across the wood floor in socked feet. She ran to him and threw her arms around him in a tight hug, all the while speaking a mile a minute.

"Stokely! I was so worried about you. Are you ok? How do your legs feel? Does your chest feel funny? Can you breathe ok? Does your head hurt?"

His legs started shaking. He sat heavily on the floor and Virginia joined him. He ran his hand over her chin and she smiled at him. "I'm fine. But you…you're ok?"

She nodded. "Sure, fine. I've had worse. You're the one who had it bad. You're so…fragile."

He put his head in his hands. "That man, Tony, he took Sam. I didn't do anything. He just took her and I didn't do anything to stop him."

Virginia shook her head and put her arm around his shoulder. "You did fine. We'll get her back. Adja's already found them. We were just waiting for you to wake up before we left. She'll be fine."

Stokely put his hands in his lap and stared at her. "You've met him before, haven't you? You know each other. Is that why he took her? He's angry with you or something?"

She wore a pained expression on her face. "I've met him before, yes. I think the Tony you've seen is younger than when I first met him; last week was his first time meeting me. The first time I saw him—he attacked me. I didn't know why. It was a long time ago. I had only been traveling a little while. He's the one who…"

She looked at her left arm and didn't say anything more.

Adja stood. "I will go tell the others you are awake. Lee has taken Cass back home. We will leave shortly."

She quietly left the room. Virginia went over to the mantle and stood with her back to Stokely. "Do you want me to take you back to Paris or do you want to stay here?"

Stokely said, "I'm coming with you. I want to help rescue Sam. I need—"

Virginia cut him off. "No. I can't lose you. You aren't coming."

Stokely was about to protest when a voice came from the doorway, "A shot of nanos would protect him from harm."

They both turned to see another Virginia, standing with arms crossed leaning against the doorjamb. She wore a black skirt with a deep purple blouse. Her hair was up in a French twist and pearls decorated her throat. Hooked over one arm was a brown leather bag. Even though the two Virginias looked the same in the face, this other one seemed years older to Stokely simply because of her manner of dress. She walked slowly into the room, high heels clicking on the wood floor.

"Tony had figured you had nanos, now he knows you don't, so he won't be expecting it."

Stokely's chronologically correct Virginia turned to him and said, "That's why he electrocuted you. If the school gets shocked they're fried. And if they're fried, no healing from a bullet to the brain."

"School?"

"Sorry, school of nanos."

The other Virginia smiled. "School of nanos, flock of drones, herd of robots..."

The Virginias looked at him. He shrugged his shoulders. "Alright."

The other Virginia pulled out a glass case that held a syringe. She handed it to Stokely's Virginia before heading to the couch. She slipped off her high heels, dangling them from one hand as she cocked her head and watched Virginia inject Stokely.

"You're so young."

"Of course he's young. He's only just started traveling with me."

"Not him. You. You act all in charge when you're scared. It's funny."

Virginia furrowed her brow and said tersely, "I do not."

"Yes, you do." The other her had a coy smile on her face, obviously finding amusement in her younger self's annoyance. It was a literal back-in-my-day moment.

"Aren't you starting to feel uncomfortable?"

"Yes, I suppose I am."

"Well why don't you go somewhere? Unless you have something important to tell me?"

"You could leave just as easily as I can."

The two stared at each other, the younger clearly weighing the humor in causing her older self discomfort and the knowledge that one day it would be her in that same spot. In a huff, she made for the door. "I'm going to talk with the others. Stokely you don't need to do that, it's fine."

He had been applying pressure to where she'd given him the shot in the crook of his elbow. Removing his thumb he saw she was right, there was no puncture mark on his skin. He stared at the other Virginia with trepidation.

"So you're an older Virginia?"

She nodded.

"How much older are you?"

She shrugged. "Who knows? I don't."

"So you know, do you know—is Sam ok?"

She nodded again. "Yes, she's fine. You'll find her and everything will be all right. She's much more capable than you're giving her credit for. She's not some helpless damsel, you know."

Stokely sat on the couch next to her. "But, I should have protected her, done something. That's what I'm supposed to do."

She laughed a little. "That's an old way of looking at things."

They sat quietly for a bit. Stokely hesitantly asked her, "Will we, will we have to stop this guy?"

"You mean will you have to kill him? No, although it would make things easier if you had. Oh, don't look so surprised. He's a killer. He enjoys hurting women. He would kill Sam in a heartbeat, he doesn't get the chance, but he would."

"You said you had met him before—that he attacked you. What...what happened?"

"He dies in an accident that I cause, a very bad one. I felt horrible about it then, but I didn't know about his... extracurricular activities at the time. Now I'm rather glad it happened."

They were quiet for a moment, the older friend observing the younger with an insightful gaze.

"This won't be the last time you encounter him."

They heard the sound of clomping footsteps at the door. Stokely's Virginia stood there, wearing heavy black boots, jeans, and a black t-shirt. Her hair was up for the first time, pulled back in a neat braided bun. She looked ready to fight.

She talked to Stokely, ignoring the other her, "We're going, come on."

Older Virginia lightly touched his hand as he stood. "Don't worry, it'll be fine. I promise."

As Stokely made his way to the door he heard a crackling noise behind him. Looking over his shoulder, he saw the older Virginia had gone.

They headed to the kitchen where the rest of the group waited. Everyone was similarly dressed, in jeans, boots, and simple t-shirts. Hunter projected a map onto the kitchen table with his computer arm, which showed a small island in the middle of a river. Labels popped up, showing a place called Petty's Island located on the Delaware River.

Adja pointed to the far right side of the island. "They're here, in the only building left on the island, April 17th 1964. We're going in pairs. Hunter with Lee, Sagitta with me, Stokely you go with Virginia. Wait until we are all there to confront him. You should try to get as close to 7 a.m. as possible."

Everyone passed around a box of black gloves. Civic-Lee explained, "These will protect you, along with the shoes, in case he tries to electrocute us."

The gloves felt rubbery, only thinner and lighter. There was a pair of boots for Stokely as well. When he slipped them onto his feet he felt the insides contract to fit him properly.

Adja spoke up. "Everyone, be cautious. Tony might be from the 1920's but he's got technologies from about the 2050's I'd guess. According to the information I have on him, he doesn't travel farther forward than about 1996. He might have another tempusnaut friend helping him."

Everyone began pairing up. Virginia wrapped her arms around Stokely's waist. "You focus on the distance and I'll get us to the right time, ok?"

He nodded. They had already done this before several times. He closed his eyes and pictured the island he had seen on the map. Lights splashed across his vision and his ears rang. The world shifted slightly and they were somewhere, somewhen else. Looking around he saw trees, running water, the sun just starting to rise in the distance. Virginia dropped her arms from around him.

"I think we got here first. We're early, we'll have to wait," She pinched the bridge of her nose, "I think for about an hour."

"How did Adja find this place? How'd she know when we needed to go to?"

Virginia shrugged. "Dunno. Probably someone in the future told her. I know she's friendly with some government or another in a couple hundred years. She will be involved with the public finally finding out about tempusnauts."

They looked around, trying to walk quietly and stay hidden amongst the island's numerous trees. They found a gravel road, pockmarked and in general disrepair with weeds growing on it here and there. Several caved in or burned out structures dotted the lane. As far as they could see there was only one building left, an old shed without any windows, large enough to hold big equipment. They assumed Tony and Sam would be there.

They circled around the building to get a better look, making sure to stay hidden among the trees. There were two doors, one in the front and one in the back sealed with a heavy, rusted, padlock. In addition, there were two large, rolling garage doors that looked as if they hadn't been opened in some time.

After waiting for what seemed like an eternity, they heard a distant pop and Hunter and Lee appeared just ahead of the trees in front of the building. Adja and Sagitta appeared a second later next to the door. A half second later Stokely heard a soft, barely audible click. Lee disappeared with another loud pop. The other three in the clearing looked around in apparent confusion. Sag staggered a bit before falling to his knees. A dark red stain bloomed on his chest. Hunter, blood running down his shoulder, ran over to his brother. Adja limped over to the pair. Stokely could see something metal protruding from a wound on her leg. He was about to go to them when Virginia stopped him.

"We'll get shot too if we go out there. Whatever it is, it can't see around the trees."

Hunter stood, dragging Sagitta up with him. His whole body shimmered for a second before he staggered back and the two of them fell to the ground.

"Whatever it was that shot them, it's keeping them from traveling. There's probably more of those things in the building."

"So how do we get inside?"

Lee suddenly appeared next to them, staggering a bit. There was a tiny cut on her cheek, which healed in a few seconds. She looked down at herself and said, "Guess I didn't get hit? What's going on?"

Virginia nodded to her. "The others did. He's got way more advanced tech than we thought. They got shot with something that's short-circuiting their jumping. He's probably got the whole building covered. We need to knock out those guns before we can get inside."

"Where the hell did he get tech like that? I thought he hadn't traveled that far? That sounds like something from *my* time!" Lee said, an angry hiss to her voice.

The three of them peeked around the trees to see the others. Adja, Hunter, and Sagitta hadn't moved. The areas on their bodies around their wounds looked strange. A slowly spreading patch of skin on each of them shimmered, fading in and out like a flickering light. The metal piece sticking from Adja's leg also shimmered.

Lee's eyes widened. "We'd call those jammers. They could kill them!"

Virginia started pacing back and forth, holding her forehead and talking. "Ok, ok. I can fix this. Just have to concentrate, bring the things I want, leave the other stuff. Ok, ok."

She sounded like someone psyching herself up to do something that she didn't want to do. She paused, looking Stokely straight in the eye, before saying once again, "Ok."

She vanished, the familiar crackling noise ringing in Stokely's ears. Barely half a minute later, she re-appeared with all three of them. One hand holding onto Adja and the other Sagitta, who still had a hold of Hunter. Stokely had never seen her or anyone travel with more than one passenger before. Virginia staggered forward several steps and Stokely caught her before her knees buckled. He could see a burst blood vessel in one of her eyes and her skin had gone shock white. Whatever she had done, it didn't look like it was good for her.

She gasped at him, "I'm all right, check on the others."

Lee already tended to Sagitta, who lay on the ground. He seemed to be unconscious, eyes closed, his breathing coming in loud gasps. Lee pulled up his shirt to reveal a large hole ripped in the middle of his chest.

Hunter sat down heavily on the ground next to his brother. "It's ok. He'll be alright."

Stokely could see the wound on Hunter's shoulder already closing up, the skin quickly growing back. Turning to Adja he saw her leg also healing quickly, the metal piece previously embedded in her no longer there. Peaking around the trees, he saw several bloody metal tubes with barbed ends lying on the ground. Virginia had teleported their friends but not the jammers inside their bodies. Stokely hadn't known such a thing was possible.

Hunter fished around in his pockets, pulling out a small black bag and a tiny metal dragonfly. He upended the bag and dozens of tiny floating metal arrow tips spilled out. They buzzed around the air in a V formation, like a flock of birds. Hunter pulled up the computer in his arm and started punching things into the keyboard.

"This should solve one problem," he said as the metal tips all flew off in different directions. The guns surrounding the building began firing furiously, hitting several of the projectiles and causing them to explode in midair. Most of the arrow tips found their marks, smashing into the guns and bursting into flames.

"And another problem." Hunter released the tiny mechanical dragonfly, which zoomed off towards the building. A minute later, Hunter brought up a holographic map with his arm, showing the interior of the shed. A large, sparsely furnished room. In one corner stood a long table next to a set of shelves. In the opposite corner, a pit of some sort. The hologram also showed blurred human figures, their features barely discernible. One, presumably Tony, was dragging the other towards the table.

Virginia said, "I'll go in first and—"

Hunter cut her off with a shake of his head. "No way, V. One of us can do that. After that stunt you just pulled, you shouldn't be going anywhere or anywhen for a while. I'm surprised you didn't pass out."

Virginia didn't say anything, but from the look on her face, Stokely didn't think she would be likely to heed Hunter's command.

Lee bent down and took Sagitta's hand. "I'll take him back to his time. Be back in a—"

Another her appeared before she could finish the sentence. The original disappeared along with

Sagitta. The newly arrived Lee nodded at Hunter. "He's at home."

Someone in the shed screamed, drawing all of their attention.

Virginia turned to Hunter. "You sure you got all the guns on the outside?"

He shrugged. "Probably?"

"Good enough for government work. On the count of three, Lee you take Stokely with you, get right next to them. The rest of us will go in through the door. Ready? One, two, three!"

Lee grabbed Stokely tightly as the others ran towards the door. It was a strange jump through space. Stokely was completely unprepared, Lee having total control over where and when they went. The world spun around them and suddenly slammed to a stand-still. Stokely staggered a bit, trying to get his bearings. The room they found themselves in looked just like the hologram Hunter had shown them. The furniture was rough hewn and worn looking, the floor just swept dirt.

Lee was already moving towards Tony, who stood in front of the long table where Sam was tied down, a gag in her mouth. She shimmered every few seconds, one of the metal devices protruding from her arm.

Lee side swept Tony, knocking him off his feet. He pulled a knife on her, dragging it through her torso. Even with blood pouring down her side, she was quick enough to grab the knife from Tony, breaking his hand in the process. Her fighting was fast and fluid, like a dancer.

Stokely ran to Sam, grabbed the metal sticking from her arm and yanked it out. She gave a muffled scream through her gag. He shouted at her, "GO!"

She shimmered slightly before disappearing.

He tried to follow but something yanked him back, a pain running through his head for a second. He gasped and fell to his knees. There was an odd numbing sensation running along his spine. He ran his hand along his back and felt slick warm blood. Looking up, he saw a strange gun hanging off the ceiling. It rotated around and seemed to track people as they moved throughout the room. He'd been shot with a jammer.

Hunter's drones hadn't taken out all the guns, apparently. Stokely couldn't feel the end of the metal sticking out of his skin, which meant he couldn't pull it out on his own.

It seemed to Stokely that time was moving incredibly fast, but in reality only about a minute had passed since he and Lee had appeared in the shed.

The front door suddenly burst open, Virginia ran in first. The gun swiveled to point at her but she disappeared before it could fire. She re-appeared next to Tony, who was still grappling with Lee.

Lee smashed her palm into Tony's face, breaking his nose. He made a grab for her but she disappeared, reappearing almost instantly behind him. She slammed her fist into the nape of his neck knocking him down, before disappearing again. Virginia kicked him hard in the side while he lay on the ground. He yelled unintelligibly and drove a knife through Virginia's boot. She screamed and fell back, her foot momentarily pinned to the floor.

The gun on the ceiling swiveled around, trying and failing to shoot Adja and Hunter as they appeared in the open door. Tony pointed at Stokely, causing the gun to swing around to face him instead. Stokely froze, stupidly staring down the barrel, unable to move. As the trigger clicked a Virginia appeared in front of Stokely. The Virginia still pinned stared for a second before disappearing, the knife dropping to the floor.

Virginia fell back against Stokely. The automated gun had hit her twice, once in the stomach and once in her fake left arm. She pulled out the jammer from her belly and dropped it on the floor. The metal embedded in her arm was not so easy to remove. It wedged in lengthwise and the barbed end seemed to be caught on the interior of the prosthetic. Virginia couldn't pull it out no matter how hard she tugged.

The gun had gone back to shooting at Hunter and Adja. Hunter threw a few more of the floating tips towards it but it shot them all out of the air. While the autonomous gun was distracted with shooting at Hunter's weapons, Adja appeared next to it in mid air, grabbed onto the machine and disappeared with it.

Lee reappeared right then, directly in front of Tony. He grabbed her throat, crushing her windpipe.

Hunter ran at him yelling, "Put her down!"

Tony threw Lee aside, sending her sprawling on the floor, gasping for air. He pulled another knife out (he seemed to have an endless supply), and hurled it at Hunter where it hit him in the dead center of his chest. He crumpled like a rag doll.

Sam re-appeared then, looking confused and shaken. She still had the ties on her wrists that once held her to the table. Tony didn't seem to notice her sudden appearance as he towered over Hunter.

Thinking on her feet, Sam grabbed the metal rod that had previously been in Virginia's stomach. She crouched low to the ground and snuck up behind Tony. He peered around the room, preparing for the next attack, when she jammed the metal between his shoulder blades. She felt the fabric of his shirt rip and blood oozed between her fingers, but she refused to let go.

Tony screamed and whirled around, smacking Sam in the face. Rage clouded Stokely's mind as he ran full force at Tony and tackled him to the ground. They wrestled on the floor for a minute before Stokely pinned Tony. Virginia grabbed some rope off the table and tied Tony's hands behind his back, a jammer wedged into his skin. She kicked him once in the stomach before walking over to Sam and pulling her into a tight hug.

Lee crouched near Hunter, gingerly pulling out the knife from his chest. She looked towards the others and said, "I'm going to take him back. Be back in a sec'."

Virginia shook her head. "Don't. We'll be along in a minute. Just need to finish up here."

Lee nodded before disappearing with her husband. Virginia went to Stokely, helping him up off the floor.

"You ok, kid?"

He nodded.

Tony lay silent on the floor. Every few seconds he flickered slightly. His face contorted with rage and hate.

Virginia carefully pressed on the wrist of her damaged arm and then tapped a sequence onto the watch faces. It clicked and her broken prosthetic detached just below the elbow. She grabbed a knife off the floor and used it to pry out the weapon stuck in the arm. She dropped the knife and metal to the floor before wrapping her good arm around Sam's shoulder.

From the floor Tony called out, "Hey! Bitch! You gonna kill me or what?"

Virginia turned to him, quiet anger written plainly across her face. She dropped her arm from around Sam and walked over to where Tony lay. She crouched, leaning in very close to his face and said in a low voice, barely audible to the others, "You're already dead, asshole. It doesn't happen here, but it will and soon."

He made a useless lunge at her. She backed away and went to her friends. "Think you can get back on your own Stokes? I'll go with Sam."

From behind them Tony began to scream in frustration.

Chapter 8 – Lessons

Several weeks after the horrendous beach trip Stokely, Sam, and Virginia headed to Virginia's home in the countryside of Georgia in 2062. They went so Virginia could finally fulfill her promise of giving them lessons on how to better control their time traveling abilities.

Stokely had been practicing his abilities while the three friends recuperated at the Plicard's family home in the 1980's. He felt more confident in his abilities, becoming more precise in his jumping. He found he ended up, on his own, within a week of when he wanted. His spacial awareness proved considerably more exact; He arrived within a few feet of where he wanted. He could also move vast distances, thousands of miles, much more than many of the other travelers he knew.

Sam wasn't progressing as quickly as Stokely with her skills, and it frustrated her. She had yet to travel anywhere or when on her own and actually arrive where she wanted. She'd also started having nightmares, which caused her to travel in her sleep. She never went very far, maybe a few hours or a day at most and typically somewhere in the house or the surrounding yard. Even though she didn't seem to be in any immediate danger from her midnight wanderings, waking up somewhere unfamiliar still scared her.

The lands contained a large old farmhouse, a barn, and several dilapidated buildings in back as well as a large pool. Automated machines tended to the surrounding fields of wheat and rye. The trio almost never saw anyone else during their time on the farm.

The second day, Virginia took Stokely and Sam out to the barn. Several mattresses lay on the ground under a long rope hanging from the ceiling. Virginia grabbed a hold of the rope before climbing up the ladder to the hayloft. The other two followed her.

"This is going to be a lesson on motion. It can be a very important thing to consider when you travel. I want you to watch me closely and then tell me what you see."

Holding tight to the rope Virginia swung out into the empty space. Just as she hit the upswing on the opposite side she vanished. After about a minute she re-appeared in the dead center of the space. She fell to the mattresses with a light thump. She hauled herself up and stood in the middle of the room holding onto the rope.

"Ok. What did you see?"

The pair looked at each other. Sam spoke up first.

"You only went a minute or two?"

Virginia shook her head. "No, not that. "

"You appeared in the center of the room?"

"Not exactly what I was talking about, but something else pertaining to it."

Stokely thought, his fingers tapping on his chin as he looked down at the mattresses. "You…you kept moving for a second or two. When you landed you weren't in the center of the room. Even though you appeared in the center you kept moving forward, like you were still swinging on the rope."

"Bingo! Winner, winner, chicken dinner."

Sam said, "Your momentum continued after you jumped. Acceleration isn't negated by traveling."

Virginia nodded. "Very good. Most of the time when we travel we are stationary so you don't really notice. But it is very important for several reasons. First, acceleration as an injury inducer. Say you are traveling in a car going sixty miles an hour. You travel out of that car. Your acceleration is still going to be sixty miles an hour until an outside force acts upon you, most likely the ground. To prevent serious bodily injury you need to slow yourself down. For example by changing your orientation as you fall."

Virginia climbed up the rope until she reached the beam it was anchored to. When she reached the top she let go, plummeting back to the ground. At the last second she disappeared again. When she reappeared she was upside down. It looked like her body moved in slow motion for a few seconds, falling towards the ceiling instead of the floor. She vanished again and reappeared a minute later right side up just a foot or so above the mattress. She laughed as she stood up this time, cheeks slightly flushed.

"Ok, so did you get that? What did I do? Sam?"

"Um. You slowed your descent by changing the way you fell. You fell up for a bit. It slowed you down."

Virginia nodded. "Yep."

Virginia climbed back up the ladder and led the other two over to the large open door of the hayloft. It looked out over a twelve-foot drop. Virginia consulted her blue watch, the only one that actually told the current time. She pointed towards the pool.

"So, another way to defer momentum when you aren't going quite so fast. Say you are running, or maybe jump off something less than twenty feet high. Water isn't deadly to fall into if you aren't falling super fast."

Sam asked, "How quickly do you reach terminal velocity?"

Virginia smiled. "About twelve to fourteen seconds. It's about two-hundred miles an hour or three-hundred-twenty-five kilometers. Although with us, you could be falling faster than terminal velocity and then slow down as you fall."

Stokely exclaimed, "Wait, what? You slow down as you fall?"

"You can only fall so fast, because of drag, friction, and all that. So if you are moving faster than you can fall you will slow down. Say if you were in a plane going six hundred miles an hour, three times what terminal velocity is, you would still be going that fast if you teleported out of the plane. If you appeared a few miles up in empty sky and oriented yourself to face the earth, that is to say instead of moving forward you are now moving towards the earth, you would be moving at the speed of when you were in the plane. After a few seconds the force of the wind would slow you down. This is all hypothetical of course, I've never heard of anyone actually doing anything like that."

She looked at her watch again.

Stokely asked, "How fast is too fast to land in water? Like bike-riding-fast, or car-fast?"

Virginia opened her mouth to answer and stopped. She hmmed and touched her finger to her lips. "You know, that is a good question. I always thought of it in heights, not in speed. I'll have to look it up. The most I'd do is sixty feet of jump, fifty feet of water."

At that second another Sam, wearing identical shorts and a tank top as the Sam in the hayloft, appeared above the pool and fell into the water with a scream. When she surfaced she yelled, "Virginia, that was not funny!"

"In emergencies, water landings are a good bet. Just don't appear in the water, appear above it," Virginia said, matter-of-fact.

"Why not?"

"Drowning, for one. But, mostly because when you appear a bit of atmosphere travels with you. Potentially, you could appear with a bubble of air, and a collapsing bubble of air underwater could be dangerous. The mantis shrimp actually uses this technique, sonoluminescence, to hunt. Good luck!"

She shoved Sam out of the open door of the hayloft. Sam screamed as she fell towards the ground before disappearing. The Sam in the pool swam to the side and hauled herself out. As she stood up she shot Virginia a death stare.

Stokely and Virginia climbed down the ladder and went out into the yard. Sam stood with her arms crossed, water pooling at her feet. "That was not funny. Don't ever do that again."

Virginia laughed a bit. "Sorry, sorry. I knew that would happen. I told me so, I knew you wouldn't get hurt. But it was good. See...I've never seen you travel in an emergency before. It was a split second decision. We already know Super-Stokes here can travel faster than a speeding bullet. Now we know you can travel faster than a twelve-foot fall."

Virginia still giggled to herself while she ran back into the barn. Sam and Stokely followed her at a slower pace. When they were all back up on the hayloft, Virginia handed the rope to Stokely.

"Ok, I want the both of you to swing out just like I did. I want you to feel what it's like. Don't miss the mattresses."

Stokely took a deep breath and stepped to the edge of the platform

He jumped, swinging through the air. Just before he went one full swing he jumped through time.

Instead of appearing in the middle of the room he materialized in the hayloft, directly in front of his friends. He crashed into them, sending everyone sprawling into the hay heaped on the floor. Sam and Virginia laughed so hard they couldn't stand up, and Stokely wore a scowl on his face that gradually turned into a sheepish grin.

When Virginia got her breath back she said, "Ok, ok. So that wasn't as accurate as I had thought it would be. But that's ok. You just need more practice. And I think not having your feet on the ground makes it much harder to concentrate. How did that seem to you?"

He thought a second while the girls pulled the hay out of their hair. "I think I got the time ok? I don't think I was gone too long."

"About ten minutes. Not bad."

"Yeah. Well it was confusing, not being able to feel the ground. And I felt, like, like something stopped me? It's hard to describe. Like when someone comes up behind you and you kinda know they're there even though you haven't turned around yet."

"That sounds like proprioception. You were aware of the walls of the barn. Without that you could arrive in the wall, which is bad. Ok, Sam your turn."

Sam nervously grabbed the rope Stokely brought to her. She stepped to the edge of the floor and looked out. "Um…you sure this is ok? What if I miss the mattresses and break my leg?"

Virginia shook her head. "You got nanos now. It will heal."

She was right of course. Sam had been outfitted with her own nanos while they were all recuperating from the fight with Tony. But that still didn't make Sam feel totally confident.

She took a deep breath and jumped. She disappeared a little too quickly, just before she hit the middle of the room. She reappeared in almost the same spot in the air. She fell to the mattresses with a soft thump. Overhead Virginia clapped her hands.

"Good! Good, you got right in the middle of the room. That's hard to do. And you jumped about thirty seconds. Very good."

Sam smiled.

"Ok, I want the two of you to practice that for the rest of the afternoon. I want you to get comfortable with it. You should also try jumping out the hayloft and landing in the pool."

They spent the rest of the day training. The pool made Stokely very wary. He didn't want to land in the deep end because of his inability to swim. After several halted tries, Sam finally decided to simply sit next to the water so she could jump in and haul Stokely out. This was fairly easy since she had several inches of height on him and had trained as a lifeguard.

They spent the next day going over precise control of arrival time. Stokely and Sam took turns disappearing and attempting to reappear at exact instances in the future. Virginia stood with a stopwatch calling out intervals (55 seconds, 11 minutes, etc.) and timed the other two to see how accurately they arrived at the preordained moment.

Stokely aimed with the least accuracy. Every once in awhile he would get lucky and appear almost perfectly when he wanted, but for the most part he had a wobble of up to fifteen minutes.

Sam jumped spot on almost from the get go. After a full day's practice she appeared within five seconds of when she wanted, amazingly accurate, according to Virginia.

As the three of them lounged next to the pool during a break, sipping soda and watching the sunset, Virginia said, "I think you're gonna need to train with Lee. She's one of the best travelers I know, she could teach you better than I can. You're already better than me and you've only been doing this a little while."

This surprised the other two. Sam asked, "How do you know we are better than you?"

She shrugged. "I have a wobble of about three minutes most of the time. Sam, yours is already down to five seconds. With practice I bet you could get it even more precise, maybe one or two seconds. Lee can do that, she's amazing."

Stokely swung his feet into the pool and splashed the water. "You seemed pretty precise when you first met me. Remember, you showed up right as I was asking you to prove time travel was real."

She shrugged again. "Sometimes we get closer than others."

"Well, Sam might be getting better, but I'm not."

She scooted over to him and stuck her own feet in the water. "You can travel far. Really far. Much farther than me. You could be a CC technician if you wanted."

"What's a CC technician?"

She laid down and held a hand up to the sky. "Chronological Correction Technician. On the inter-planetary shuttles in the future, the ships that travel between planets, they have an organic time traveler on staff. The trips between planets take hundreds of years, so they use organic travelers to make the journey go faster, jumping millions of miles when they're out in interstellar space with nothing near to accidentally run into. When they get closer to their destination planet they go back in time to negate the travel time."

Sam spoke up, "They move an entire ship?"

"Not alone. It's a combination of the organic traveler and an integrated mechanical time machine system that's built into the ship. The organic traveler basically steers. Like, you can have a race car that goes three-hundred miles per hour but a professional racer is going to get more out of it than a regular person."

"What about the people on the ship? Is it like a generation ship?"

"Nope. The passengers are in cryo sleep. The staff doesn't age. Some ships, they're also in cryo sleep with an uplink to a mechanical body, others their bodies are augmented or outright designed from birth to give 'em an unnaturally long life."

Stokely looked confused. "From birth? Like eugenics?"

Virginia propped herself up on her elbows. "Sorry Stokely, you're so chill about all this I forget sometimes I should be giving you a primer. There are some similarities with the eugenics movements you would be familiar with. Instead of sterilizing, or telling the population who can and cannot reproduce, people in the future have their reproductive material reprogrammed. It doesn't have to affect their own bodies, just their potential children's."

Sam spoke up, "So, they could weed out problems? Instead of testing a fetus in utero, any problems are fixed before the baby is even conceived?"

"That's the idea. It doesn't always work so neatly though."

The sun had fully set to reveal a night sky full of twinkling stars, winking their faint glows. The Milky Way was barely visible, a streak dashed across the black.

"There were still some problems, unforeseen outcomes. And not everyone thinks it's a good idea, different planets have different rules. I've got a few books on the history of it if you wanna read about it."

Virginia grew quiet, gently splashing the water with her feet.

Sam scooted over to her and lay down as well before asking, "What do you think of gene manipulation?"

Virginia shrugged a bit. "Personally I think sometimes societies in the future teeter precariously close to those systems of old. Eventually the problems with gene-manip are righted but it takes a very long time. It's hard to see in the long run what humanity is losing by taking away what we assume is lesser. What do you two think of it?"

Stokely spoke up immediately, "It's wrong. It's playing god."

Sam shook her head. "I dunno. Pretty much any medical advancement could be called playing god, right? We've eradicated, what? Four, five diseases from the world? That's messing with nature in a big way."

Virginia spoke up, "From your time Sam it's seven; two are in cattle, five in humans. In Stokely's time it would be none."

Sam's eyes widened. "Oh, yeah. I forget how different it is when you're from Stokes."

Stokely asked curiously, "What do they get rid of?"

Sam spoke up. "Smallpox. I know that one, my great granddad use to tell me about it. And, um, the one that paralyzed people."

"Polio. I got vaccinated for that one. My aunt had it when she was a kid."

Virginia said, "Guinea worm, measles—"

"I had that as a kid," Stokely cut in.

"Yaws, rinderpest, and mad cow."

Sam said. "I've heard of that one, the mad cow. There was an outbreak when my dad was a kid, we learned about it in school. And malaria is almost gone right?"

Virginia nodded. "Yep, although it's never really gone, gone. Humans aren't the only vector, so it still crops up from time to time."

Stokely turned to Sam. "What do you think of eugenics? Or what's it called, gene manipulation?"

Sam looked out at the stars and answered in a quiet voice. "Well, I can see why it could be good. Imagine never having to worry about getting cancer, or dementia."

Virginia opened her eyes and stretched a hand towards the sky. "None of the Pilchard kids have gene-manip, everything left to chance."

Stokely turned to Virginia. "Do you?"

"Do I what?"

"Have gene-manip?"

She laughed. "No way dude. We didn't have that when I was born. Believe it or not, but most of this stuff was just as unknown for me not that long ago."

Stokely looked up and out at the stars. "It's all so strange."

Sam nodded in agreement. "Yeah, it's like being in a comic book."

Stokely looked over at Virginia and asked, "What's the most different for you, Virginia?"

She quietly thought for a moment before answering. "The noise."

Stokely almost asked her what she meant when she suddenly sat up and jumped in the pool, splashing the other two with warm water. They watched her swim to the bottom of the deep end.

Sam shook her head. "She's an enigma inside a riddle wrapped in a firewall, isn't she?"

She slid into the water silently, gracefully gliding towards Virginia. Stokely stared up at the bright stars, listening to the sounds of his friends splashing and laughing.

Chapter 9 – The Curious Incident With the Girl in the Night

The house was quiet, save for the pitter-patter of rain on the roof.

Stokely sat at the kitchen table, unable to sleep. He suffered from chrono-lag, the time traveler's equivalent to jetlag. Delphi the cat, who had been procured from their French home and brought to San Francisco, curled up in his lap. He had decided to read instead of lying on his bed, staring up at the ceiling. There was a stack of books on the table that he leafed through. *The Time Machine*, *The Hitchhiker's Guide to the Galaxy*, *A Brief History of Time*. He settled on *A Wrinkle in Time*. It was a book he had heard of, published a few years before he went traveling.

"It was a dark and stormy night."

He had read the line before many times, in an old novel called Paul Clifford. He knew somewhere—out in the world—was the old dog-eared copy that his uncle had given him. The book in his hands was very different.

Suddenly, there was a cackling sound, like electricity coming off a wool sweater and the room filled with the smell of ozone. From behind him there was a sharp intake of air. He turned around.

Virginia was standing in a puddle of water, soaking-wet hair tangled around her shoulders like a net. She clutched something in her hands, a dark matted ball of fabric. She was clutching it so tight her knuckles were white.

Stokely jumped out of the chair, Delphi tumbling to the floor with an annoyed look.

"Virginia, what's going on? What happened?" he demanded.

Her eyes were large saucers, staring at him. Her mouth was slightly open but no sound came out. He wondered if she was sleepwalking, if she had managed to travel somewhen and back without waking up. He ran and got towels from the hall closet. When he returned to the kitchen she was still standing, staring into space. Stokely wrapped her in a towel and sat her in a chair while he cleaned up the puddle. When he was done he pulled up a chair next to Virginia and sat down.

As the shock of her sudden appearance left him, he noticed the cut on her head. It was just at her temple, blood slowly oozing down her cheek. Stokely dabbed at it with a dishcloth. She blinked slowly at him, and was becoming more aware of her surroundings.

"Stokely."

He nodded. "Yeah. Are you ok? What happened?"

She looked down at the fabric in her hands. She uncurled her fingers, letting it fall to the floor. Delphi walked over to sniff it and, apparently finding it not to her liking, hissed.

"I'm ok."

Stokely picked up the fabric, which was also soaking wet, and squeezed it out over the sink. He held it up and saw it was a navy blue, long sleeved shirt. There was a slit down the front, as if it were a jacket, but there were no buttons or zipper.

"What's this?" he asked turning to face Virginia.

"It's yours."

Stokely didn't like anything about the present situation. Virginia's short answers, her glazed eyes, the wound on her face. He had a bad feeling in the pit of his stomach.

Tossing the shirt in the sink, he grabbed her arm and got her to her feet. "Come on, let's get you to bed. You'll feel better after you sleep. You can tell me what's up in the morning."

As he led her towards the stairs she stopped.

"I can't. I'm upstairs."

So this wasn't the current Virginia. He wondered when she was from. He steered her to the living room and to the couch. Her clothes, some kind of future fabric, were already dry. As he was toweling off her hair she wrapped her arms around his thin frame. She began sobbing, holding onto him tightly. He gently hugged her.

"Hey, hey. It's all right. What's wrong? What happened?"

With her face pressed against his chest she shook her head.

"I'm sorry, I'm sorry. I can't. I couldn't."

That was as much as he could understand. She started crying even harder, her breath coming in gasps. After a few minutes she quieted and pulled away from him. Stokely noticed how tired she looked. Dark circles lined her eyes and she was swaying on her feet. He was holding onto her left arm, his hand wrapped around her wrist. There was no pulse.

"Virginia, is your arm broken? It has no pulse."

She shook her head. "It's fine. Don't worry about it."

"You need to sleep."

"Can you stay here?"

He nodded. She lay down on the couch and he curled up on the large love seat, with his feet propped up on an ottoman. She fell asleep almost immediately, her chest moving in a steady rise and fall.

He lay awake for several hours watching her, before he finally nodded off.

In the morning, he woke with a start to see that she was already gone, only a small indent in the pillow was left to show she had been there.

****

A few days later, as the trio of friends were sitting down for dinner, Virginia lightly touched Stokely on the arm.

"Hey, Stokes, are you alright? You've seemed down."

He looked from Sam to Virginia. They both looked concerned. He hadn't told them about the strange incident with the older Virginia. He wasn't quite sure why. Maybe a part of him thought if he didn't acknowledge that something very bad seemed to be predetermined for their future it wouldn't come to pass.

"Well. You came to visit a few days ago, the night we had those thunderstorms. And you seemed...out of sorts."

As they ate, he described the whole encounter. Sam looked scared. Virginia waved her hand dismissively.

"Who knows what I'm up to. I'm not worried."

"That seriously doesn't put you on edge?"

She shrugged. "Told you. Not worried. If there's something we could do about it, I'd have told you. If there's nothing we can do, I'd rather not know ahead of time and have to think about it more than needed."

Sam crossed her arms. "You live too much in the present. You're like an animal that can't see past right now."

"And you live too much looking towards the future. You should enjoy now more."

Virginia stood up, walked over to the counter, and pulled a saucepan off the drying rack.

"What are you doing?"

"Making us some hot chocolate. If it bothers you so much I'll see if I can find an older me and ask her. Tomorrow."

Hot chocolate had become their standard bedtime ritual. She carefully measured out the powdered cocoa, put a dash of cinnamon in one cup for Sam and an extra spoonful of sugar for Stokely.

They were all much quieter than usual as they sipped their drinks, each lost in their own thoughts. Stokely quite suddenly began to feel incredibly drowsy. Sam and Virginia also began nodding off right at the kitchen table.

"What was in that hot chocolate?" he asked before quietly putting his head on the table and falling into a deep sleep. But there was no answer, for his two friends were also in a bottomless slumber.

Chapter 10 – In Which Our Tempusnauts Are Put in a Cage

The cold air smelled of bleach.

Blank, white walls greeted Stokely when he opened his eyes. He was in a simple room that contained a bed, toilet, and sink—nothing more. The wall farthest from him was made entirely of glass. Rising from the bed, he walked over to it and peered out. Stokely could see a long hall that was filled with identical rooms. Directly across from him was a surly looking older man laying on the floor of his little room, staring up at the ceiling. On either side of the man were Stokely's travel companions: Virginia on the left and Sam on the right. Sam sat on her bed with her hands pressed into her face. Virginia was standing at the glass wall of her room, staring at him intensely.

"Virginia what happened? Where are we?"

She shook her head, pointed to her ear and made an X with her arms. She gestured toward him then grabbed at a silver and white collar around her throat. Stokely touched an identical collar attached to his own neck. He hadn't noticed it before, the material was so light. Tracing his fingers all the way around to the nape of his neck, he could feel three small prongs that disappeared into his skin.

He felt ill, although he didn't know if it was from what the device was doing to him or from fear. He figured the device was the reason the small communicators he and his companions had implanted in their ears weren't working.

Taking a deep breath and telling himself he was about to do something he would wish he hadn't, Stokely prepared to jump through time and space. He focused on a spot just on the other side of the glass wall in front of him and as close to the present as he could manage. His body tensed and a ringing started in his ears, spider webs of light bled into his eyesight. At first the familiar pull began—a feeling of his body being gripped by an invisible force, but then all at once a pain seized him.

Falling forward on all fours, he thought he might puke. Fire flared in his limbs and it felt as though someone had kicked him in the head. Looking up, through streaming eyes, he could see Virginia watching him with a pained expression. She touched the fingertips of her right hand to her lips then brought the hand down to meet the fingertips of her left.

Stokely knew this gesture meant "bad," one of the few Sign Language words he could remember. He wished he had learned more than the basics. At least he knew the alphabet.

After a few minutes the feeling of nausea passed and he shakily got to his feet. Raising his right hand, index finger pointed up he wiggled it back and forth. "Where?"

Virginia shrugged and shook her head. Slowly she spelled out a word for him with her fingers. H-E-L-L.

Sam decided to take that moment to lift her head and notice him. She bounded off her bed and threw herself at the glass front of her cell. She waved frantically at him, slamming her hands against the glass and shouting. He pointed at his ear and shrugged. She nervously ran her fingers through her short hair. There would be no talking with her, certainly not out loud and not with his hands. She had never bothered to learn any Sign Language, considering it a waste of effort when there was so much translation technology at her fingertips.

Sam became visibly frustrated at his lack of understanding her frantic hand gestures. Staring very intently at him, she brought her hand to her hair and then drew it down toward her middle, palm facing up. He stared at her blankly, still not understanding.

Annoyance crept over her face as she pointed to her left arm, and then wrapped her right hand around her forearm. Clarity dawned on him. Nodding vigorously, he pointed to the left and held up his hand in the "ok" gesture.

She smiled, clearly happy to learn their companion was all right. When he looked back toward Virginia she raised an eyebrow at him and spelled out S.A.M. He nodded and gestured towards Sam's small room. Virginia nodded as well and went to sit on her bed, looking deep in thought.

Stokely sat on his own bed trying to remember what had happened. The three of them had been at Virginia's townhouse in San Francisco in the 1960's. Sam's limited jumping length meant they did not occupy the house much earlier, even though Virginia owned the place for well over a century.

They had been having dinner and then…nothing. He couldn't remember washing up or going to sleep. It was just blank. He was still wearing the same clothes as before, although his belt and shoes were gone. The same went for the girls, although he noticed Virginia still had her many assorted wristwatches strapped to her arm.

Virginia, he observed, was sitting on her bed with her back against the far wall. As he watched her, she shimmered slightly and gave a small gasp. She was trying to jump.

As the minutes passed she continued her futile efforts, shimmering in and out of sight several times. As far as Stokely could tell she wasn't making any progress. He motioned to her, spelled out S.T.O.P., but she only shook her head at him. He was worried. The collars could be doing damage. But impulsive Virginia didn't seem too concerned.

After what Stokely judged to be about an hour, a bell chimed. The others looked up at the noise. A small section of the wall slid open to reveal a cubby. Inside was a tray containing a plate with a sandwich and a bowl of soup as well as a large bottle of water. Across the hall the man grabbed the tray and sat on his bed. He began eating without hesitation. He looked familiar to Stokely, although he wasn't sure why. Catching Stokely watching him eat, the man smiled a rather humorless smile and gave a short, seated bow, bringing his hand to his head as if to tip a hat. Stokely realized he was looking at an older version of the one Pilchard he'd only ever seen in pictures.

Chamaeleon, the wayward son.

From what Cassa had told him, Chamaeleon had given up traveling and settled down to have a normal, boring life. Ursa and Solum, their mother and father, never mentioned him.

Sam looked at her food for a minute before pulling out the tray. She dumped everything on the floor before going back to her bed.

A voice spoke, presumably through a hidden speaker, "The food is safe to eat."

Virginia grabbed her tray and sat on the floor, legs sprawled. She sniffed the food with trepidation, and then bit into the sandwich gingerly. Stokely watched her slowly eat her food. When their eyes met she smiled then clutched at her throat and kneeled over. He felt a second of panic before she sat back up, laughing. He glared at her until she blew him a kiss. He shook his head. This wasn't a time for joking.

Stokely grabbed the water from his own cubby, leaving the food. Virginia might be all right with eating their captor's food but he wasn't hungry enough yet. He took a swig of the water. It seemed fine although he knew that tasteless, odorless drugs existed in most time periods.

The man Stokely presumed to be Chamaeleon had finished his food, sticking the tray and dishes back in the wall cubby. Standing next to the glass front, he seemed expectant.

After a minute or so, two soldiers and a man in a lab coat appeared. The lab-coated man waved a band on his wrist near the glass wall and it opened splitting in half, the sections disappearing into the floor and ceiling. The man in the room left with the three others, shaking off the soldiers when they grabbed his arms.

The soldiers looked to the man in the lab coat who merely shrugged and the four walked down the hall out of Stokely's line of sight.

He sat on his bed trying to figure out what time period they were in. This was definitely not the 1960's, which meant these people had the ability to travel. Touching the collar around his neck he thought back to the history books he had read.

Those were human soldiers, not autonomous robots. They must be sometime before 2170—the time when the armies of the world became predominantly robotic. The soldiers seemed to defer to the lab-coat man, whom Stokely assumed was some kind of scientist or doctor. That could mean it was during a war when the military was apt to giving scientists generous amounts of leeway and power. Sophisticated time travel wasn't until the 2080's. Stokely assumed they were before 2129 when proper laws were put in place governing time travel.

So a war between 2080 and 2129.

Most everything he could think of were brush fire wars but two were of a more serious nature: the cold war with the Moon Colony spanning the 2080's until the early 2100's, and the short but intense Tenochtitlan-Texas war which lasted from 2121 until 2123.

Lost in thought, Stokely didn't notice the three people standing at the front of his cell until the glass opened. Two soldiers and a woman in a lab coat stood before him.

"You are to come with me. Try anything and my helpers will hit you with a sedative. You are not to speak unless asked a direct question. You will be referred to as HG23 from now on. Is that clear?" The woman sounded bored as she talked. She had severe features, sharp cheekbones and ice blue eyes. Stokely could tell she was a woman use to getting what she wanted.

He stared at her, unmoving. As she advanced toward his bed Stokely could see a faint glimmer in her left eye. She was wearing a contact computer.

"I asked you a direct question. I expect an answer, HG23. Did you understand my previous instructions?"

Across the hall Virginia was watching. T.A.L.K. she spelled, as subtle as she could.

"Yes, I understood," Stokely said to the woman.

She glanced over her shoulder at Virginia. "She the ring leader, then? Figured as much. It'll be no use listening to her now. She's stuck here, same as you. The sooner you learn who's in charge the easier life will be for you. Now come with me."

As she turned and walked out of the room, the soldiers advanced on him. Grabbing his arms, they pulled him gruffly to his feet and walked him out of his cell.

Another trio were at Sam's door, the glass just beginning to move apart. Sam leapt through the widening space, landing on the man standing in front of it and hitting him repeatedly in the face before the soldiers could pull her off. She went limp after a second or two, presumably from the same sedative Stokely had been threatened with. As he was led to a door at the far end of the hall he twisted his head around to get a better look at where he was. He had enough time to count the cells (ten total) and glance at their occupants before one of the soldiers barked, "Eyes front!"

The cell next to Sam held a slender, dark-skinned man with long dark hair in two braids that watched Stokely intently. Tattoos adorned his face and hands, simple cross hatchings, lines, and dots, indicating he was from much farther back in time than originally thought. It reminded Sam of the mummies and their tattoos, done as medical treatments for various ailments. Next to Stokely's cell was a small red headed girl. She appeared childlike, perhaps eleven or twelve years old. Although, if she was a time traveler as Stokely assumed, he knew her real age could be impossible to discern. The other rooms were empty.

Exiting through a door at the far end of the hall, they continued walking down a long twisting corridor. Everything was white here and had an antiseptic feel. The corridor ended abruptly at a heavy metal door. The woman waved her wristband at the door and it opened silently.

Inside, there were several small cubicles divided by glass walls. Each area was set up like a simple doctor's office, with an examination table, wheeled chair, small white cabinet, and several medical instruments that were hung on the wall. Stokely was led to a cubicle and told to sit on the examination table. He could see the man he thought was Chamaeleon sitting in a cubicle across from him being examined by the same lab coated man as before.

His chaperone sat down on the wheeled chair. She gave him a very pointed look. "You may call me Dr. Perseco. Hold out your arm. I want to take your vitals."

He gave her a blank look and did not move. Sighing she grabbed his arm and attached a small silver metal piece that adhered to the skin of his wrist. She began tapping the air with her hands, the contact computer in her eye flashing information. "Subject HG23 appears healthy. BP 105/75. Heart rate 55. Height 1.95 meters. Weight 78 kilograms. Body fat is 10 percent. Serum iron at 100 micrograms. Vitamin D3 looks to be a little low. Will recommend a possible food supplement or a UVB light in HG23's holding cell."

As she talked to her computer and continued to type, Sam was carried into a cubicle adjacent to Stokley's. Her lanky arms were limp, her head tipped back, eyes closed. The soldier laid her on the examination table and stood at attention in the corner of the small room. The doctor Sam had attacked soon followed, holding a bloodied handkerchief to his face. He was a tall, bone thin man, young-looking but with a shock of white hair. The rest of the captive time travelers were brought in one at a time, with Virginia being last. Unlike everyone else, her hands were bound with silver metal and there were four guards on her instead of two. She flashed Stokely a grin and a wink as she walked by.

Dr. Perseco had stopped typing to watch as well. "How old is CP80?"

When Stokely didn't answer her, the Doctor tapped the band around her wrist. A sharp jolt went through Stokely's body, as if he had touched an electric fence. "I've already told you when I ask you a question you are to answer me. How old is CP80?"

Stokely shook his head. "Don't know who you're talking about."

She placed her hands together, fingertips just barely touching. "You know full well who I'm talking about. This will be a lot easier for all of us if you just cooperate with me. We have been unable to verify an estimate of your travel companion's age. You are between 20 and 27 years old. The British one, AN14, is between 23 and 29. Now tell me how old CP80 is."

Stokely gave a halfhearted shrug. "She never told me her real age. Sometimes she says she's 16 sometimes it's 900. She's an unreliable narrator."

The doctor's eyes narrowed to slits over her fingertips. "What year are you and your friends originally from?"

Stokely wondered how much information the people here knew about him and his friends. "400 B.C." Another sharp jolt went through him.

"No one could travel that far. What year are you and your friends from?"

Stokely watched several soldiers argue about something while standing in the hallway. One of them was gesturing wildly toward Virginia.

"Just before the heat death of the universe. We came back here to escape oblivion."

Stokely expected to receive another shock, but none came. Instead Dr. Perseco sighed and placed her hands in her lap.

"Look, I know this isn't easy for you, but I'm telling the truth when I say cooperating will make your life easier. We know you aren't all from the same time period. CP80 seems to have some incredibly sophisticated modifications to herself that you and AN14 lack."

Another doctor had joined the group of soldiers in the hallway. He was an older man who walked with a cane. Stokely could see that as the man spoke one side of his face remained still, as if he had had a stroke. "You think she's dangerous don't you? That's why she has so many guards on her and her hands tied."

Dr. Perseco gave him a menacing look. "I did not ask you a question. You are not permitted to speak unless given permission. I don't want to have to remind you again."

A tall blond woman joined the man with the cane. Stokely figured she was a soldier, although, unlike the others she wore a silver leaf attached to her collar. Sam was beginning to wake up as the pair walked toward Virginia, her head jerking around in confusion.

"We know she has some kind of nanomachinery in her blood system, most organic travelers we detain do. Hers, however, are in a class by themselves. The sedative we use worked half as long on her as on a normal person. If the retrieval team hadn't brought her here first she probably would have escaped. I want any information you have about her now."

Virginia suddenly grabbed the soldier nearest her, the silver ties that bound her wrists had fallen to the floor. In a split second she held the soldier's tactical knife pressed against his throat. A small drop of blood welled up next to the blade and ran down his neck. The blond woman and the man with the cane stood at the entrance to Virginia's cubical. The three appeared to be calmly talking when the blond woman quickly and coolly pulled out her sidearm and shot the soldier in the head. She motioned to one of the other soldiers, talking with him.

"I don't know anything about Virginia. She doesn't tell me anything," Stokely said, stunned by the blond woman's actions.

The soldier pulled Sam out of her room and over to Virginia's. The blond woman talked to Virginia, all the while standing with her side arm pressed against Sam's temple. Virginia gave her a hate-filled look as she handed her knife to one of the men in the room.

"Do you know if CP80's nanomachinery is from her own time period or if she had to travel to acquire it?"

"I already told you, I don't know anything about her."

Sam cried, sobbing so hard the soldier taking her back to her cubicle had to hold her up. The blond woman and the man with the cane turned to walk away. Virginia's face wore a furious expression. She flickered once, twice, three times. On her third try she disappeared.

Everyone, including Dr. Perseco, stopped what they were doing to watch. The blond woman looked behind her toward where Virginia should have been, a look of confusion on her face.

After about fifteen seconds Virginia appeared in front of Stokely. Her eyes were glassy, fixed and staring at nothing. Her body crumpled to the ground, her hands reaching out and tensing as if trying to grab at something.

"Get out of the way, she's having a seizure." Dr. Perseco pushed Stokely aside, kneeling next to Virginia. After what seemed like an eternity Virginia stilled. Two soldiers grabbed Stokely and pulled him into the hallway. The blond woman stood in front of him, her arms crossed, a sour look on her face.

The woman asked Stokely "Did she say anything to you? Give you any kind of instructions?"

When he didn't answer her she smacked him once, sharply across the face.

"Answer me!"

Stokely shook his head. "She didn't say anything to me. She was busy having a fit."

She narrowed her eyes at him, making her look like a snake watching a mouse. "Do not try me HG23. I'm in no mood, especially after your little friend there cost me one of my soldiers."

"*You* shot that soldier!"

Another jolt went through Stokely, this one lasting much longer. His knees buckled and he landed on all fours. The woman grabbed his hair, forcing his face into the ground and talking in his ear, "I have no need for uncooperative test subjects. Is that clear?"

He nodded.

She let go of his hair and stood to go. "Good. I'm glad we have an understanding. You may call me Lieutenant Colonel Phago. Aside from Doctor Campbell over there," she gestured to the man with the cane, "I am in charge here."

Dr. Campbell ambled slowly over to Stokely as two of the soldiers pulled him to his feet. The doctor examined him by shining a light in his eyes, checking his teeth. It made him feel like an animal being prepared for auction. The doctor never said a word to him, never acknowledged him in any way. He gave directions to a thin soldier with sandy blond hair.

"Take this one to my office. I would like to examine him personally."

The thin soldier led him to a blue door against the back wall. Inside was an examination room, larger and more richly furnished than the others. Instead of a rolling chair there was a high-backed leather chair and a solid oak cabinet. The walls were wood instead of glass, offering this room privacy not afforded to the rest of the facility.

The soldier motioned him to sit on the examination table.

Glancing at the door, he said quietly, "Try not to seem too interesting. Dr. Campbell isn't as nice to test subjects as the other doctors here—likes to cut people up. But he'll only take you as his personal lab rat if he thinks you're unusual. Don't piss him off either. He has a mean streak."

Stokely gave him a suspicious look. "Why would you tell me that?"

The soldier shrugged. "Just some friendly advice."

The door opened and Dr. Campbell slowly made his way inside. He seated himself in the leather chair, and gestured toward the examination table with his hand. The chair obliged him, sliding itself across the floor until it rested directly in front of Stokely.

"Let's check the vitals," he said. It wasn't directed at either Stokely or the soldier. He appeared to be giving voice commands to his contact computer. Stokely assumed it was because his right hand, much like the right side of his face, didn't work properly and talking was easier than typing.

"Everything seems to be in good working order. Testing motor functions." He tapped Stokely's knee with a small mallet, causing it to jump. "Good, good. Follow my finger with your eyes if you could. Now close your eyes and touch your nose. Yes, that's fine. If you could sit here at the edge of the table, yes feet hanging over like that. Now just relax and move with my hands." He rested his hands on either side of Stokely's face. Quickly the doctor turned Stokely's head to the left, then right before tipping him backward so he was lying down. Just as quickly, he sat him back up, turning his head side to side again. "That looks fine, balance is good. Lie down on your stomach."

Stokely did as the old man instructed.

"If you could hold his arms and legs."

Stokely thought he was talking to the soldier, but the man made no motion toward the table. Instead metal bands snaked their way around his limbs, gently yet forcefully holding him in place. Reaching into the oak cabinet the doctor pulled out a long syringe and a can of sprayable bandage.

Stokely began to struggle against the bonds. "Wait, what are you—"

The doctor cut him off with a wave of his hand. "Silence."

A metal band curled around his mouth, preventing him from speaking. Something cold touched his back, spreading a chill through his spine. He couldn't see what was happening but felt as if someone was pinching his skin. After a few moments the feeling went away and he heard the hiss of a bandage being sprayed on.

The metal bands released him. "You may sit up now. Analyze this for me. The usual tests."

A section of the wall slid open. The doctor stuck the syringe, now filled with a yellow liquid, into the cubby. Stokely rubbed his back as he sat up. He could feel the bandage being absorbed into his skin, spreading warmth.

Dr. Campbell got the faraway look in his eyes of someone reading off a contact computer screen. "Hum. Rather disappointing. No unusual body chemistry, no unusual chemical exposure. Standard broad range nano-immunizations. Smallpox vaccine administered as a live vaccinia virus. Antibodies for measles. Well it looks as though you aren't very unique as far as my tests can tell. What's your range?"

Stokely fidgeted with his hands. "Umm. Sorry, my what?" The doctor gave him a blank look, as if listening to a particularly slow child asking a question.

Speaking in an annoyed voice, he said, "Your range of time travel. Relative to the year you first started traveling from, how many years into the past and future can you travel?"

He debated whether or not he should lie to the old man. He figured the less these people knew about him the better, but they had his travel companions as leverage. That was a very good incentive to tell the truth. Also, if what Virginia had told him was true, his time traveling abilities were very average so he shouldn't have to worry about the doctor becoming too interested in him. Stokely decided to tell him a lower number than what was the truth. "Uh, about 300 years I think. Around 150 either way."

The doctor nodded. "Hmm. Better than some, but not the most extreme. You can travel through space as well, yes? What is the greatest distance you have traveled?"

"New York?"

The doctor sighed. "That is not a distance. That is a place. Where did you leave from?"

He wasn't sure what he should tell the old man, but he knew he needed to lie. He'd been told he was very good at moving through space, but he didn't know what average was. Blindly picking a city he said, "Washington, D.C."

The doctor nodded curtly. "Well you seem to be across the board average. Take him back, I'm done with him. Bring the crying one in next."

The soldier led him out the door, holding him firmly by the arm. They were met in the hall by another soldier leading Sam. The soldier dipped his head in greeting. "Hey Baines, Dr. Campbell wanted this one right?"

Baines nodded, "Yeah, thanks. I'll take her. He can go back to Dr. Perseco."

Sam gave Stokely a miserable look while the soldiers were talking. Her eyes looked red from crying. As inconspicuously as possible he mouthed act boring. As he was led away he glanced back at his friend. She also looked over her shoulder at him, with a perplexed expression on her face. He hoped she would figure out his message.

When the pair arrived back at Dr. Perseco's office the doctor read from several holograms projected in the air around her. Medical terminology Stokely couldn't understand and what appeared to be scans of different people's bodies and heads filled the holograms.

"Sit down and take off your shirt," the doctor said somewhat distractedly, gesturing toward the examination table. When Stokely made no move the soldier gruffly pushed him toward the table.

He pulled his sweater over his head and sat it on the table next to him. Dr. Perseco waved away the holograms and slid her chair over toward Stokely. She grabbed his wrist and turned it over to check the small metal piece. She gave him a very pointed look. "I was watching your vitals while you talked with Dr. Campbell. Heart rate went up, adrenalin elevated. Either you're bright enough to be afraid of him or were lying to him. I'm going to guess a bit of both. The old man might believe the threat of physical pain is enough to get cooperation from anyone but I don't. I catch you lying to me or trying anything stupid and it'll be one of your friends punished, not you. Understand me?"

Stokely nodded.

"Good. Now we are going to be doing some data gathering. That is primarily what you are here for. Lie back, I'm going to put a monitor on you."

He was expecting something similar to the small monitor already on his wrist, but the doctor pulled something different out of the cabinet. It was a black metal, diamond- shaped thing. She held it next to her wristband for a second and it started to emit a faint blue glow from the center. Leaning over Stokely she placed it on his chest.

"Hold still."

She began tapping in the air again, her contact computer flashing information. "Alright, this will sting. Take a breath and now let it out."

Four prongs slid out of the device, embedding itself in his skin. He gasped. There was a sharp burning sensation at first, which gradually subsided into an odd numbness that spread across his chest.

"Alright, everything looks good," the doctor said with a look of satisfaction. "Now, I want you to attempt to move into the future. Don't try to move to a new location. Stay seated just where you are and try to appear as close to now as you can." Stokely stared at her, unmoving. Surely it was some kind of trick. "It's alright. It won't hurt if you follow my instructions. You're not here to be tortured, you're here to be studied."

Stokely decided to try going as far into the future as he could. For him that would be November 16, 2133. Shutting his eyes and taking a deep breath, he focused on the bright, crisp morning, a large wooded park in the middle of a bustling city—escape still on the edges of his mind.

Everything began to happen as normal, spider webs of light snaking across his vision, something gripping his whole body and tugging it forward. He expected to be stopped, to feel the pain from before but it didn't come.

The scene changed, but only slightly.

For a split second he glimpsed the park, he could feel the crisp fall breeze on his face. But then he was back in the room. The doctor went from sitting in front of him to standing near the door, talking with a soldier. The pair stopped speaking when he appeared.

Dr. Perseco smiled, said, "And here he is. Looks to be 4 minutes and 36 seconds."

Stokely's head was spinning. Everything felt far away and surreal. Standing up in confusion, he wobbled on his feet. Being vertical turned out to be a mistake. His stomach jumped into his throat and he fell forward, dry heaving. He could see the doctor advancing on him before he blacked out.

Jolting awake sometime later, he found himself in a bed covered by a blue blanket. Blue curtains hung around him, shielding the rest of the room from his view. Running his hand over his chest he found the device was missing.

He sat up slowly, his head aching, the room spinning. He gingerly swung his legs over the bed. Someone had changed him into a soft hospital robe, the same blue cloth as everything else. The floor felt cold on his bare feet. When he pulled back the curtain he found himself in a large room filled with beds the same as his. The curtain was drawn on only one other bed, just next to him. A guard stood at the far end of the room, lazily flipping through holograms that were suspended in the air in front of him. Stokely could see it was Baines, the guard who had warned him before.

Next to him there came a whispered hiss, "Stokely. You still alive, man?"

A pale face peered at him from between the slit in the curtain.

"Virginia, you're ok!" Stokely whispered back. "I thought you might have died. You were so still."

Virginia very quickly and quietly crept over to Stokely's bed. Baines didn't appear to notice.

Virginia placed her hands on either side of Stokely's face for a second, examining his eyes. When she seemed satisfied she wrapped her arms around him in a hug.

"What was that for?" Stokely asked.

Letting him out of the hug and ruffling his hair in an affectionate manner she answered, "I was checking to make sure they didn't install a camera in your eye. Don't want to be spied on."

Stokely sat on his bed. His legs still felt wobbly and his head hurt. "Should I look in your eyes, too? Make sure you haven't got one?"

She shook her head. "I would know if I had one. I've already run diagnostics on myself. These things," She indicated the collar around her neck, "seem to be blocking some signals in our brains. From what I can tell it's mostly affecting the cerebrum, the cortical plate, and the apneustic center." She sat on the bed next to him.

"So you figure out how to get it off yet?" Stokely asked.

Virginia drew her knees to her chest and wrapped her arms around her legs. "No."

They sat in silence for a minute or two before Stokely said, "Well, what's the plan?"

She gave him a sideways glance. "I have no idea. If I could get to some friends in the relative future I could ask for help. It's against interplanetary accord to do experiments on organic time travelers."

"Would they arrest all the people here?"

She shook her head. "No. They might strongly suggest this place stop what they are doing, but they couldn't actually arrest anyone because the laws

161

haven't been written yet. Can't punish someone for a rule that doesn't exist."

She shut her eyes and pinched the bridge of her nose.

"You have a headache, too?" Stokely asked.

She nodded.

"So you reckon you know when we are then?"

She nodded again. "It's the tail end of the second Cold War. It'll be winding down in a few years from when I figure we are. I've heard the governments of Earth were trying to threaten the Moon with time travel, saying they were gonna go back and stop the Lunar Colony from happening. It didn't work 'cause someone tipped them off to the whole can't-change-history thing. Did you talk to that evil blond woman?"

Stokely dipped his head. "Yeah. Her name's Lieutenant Colonel Phago."

Virginia scowled. "When I get ahold of her I'm going to feed her to a dinosaur."

He laughed and she smiled.

The curtain surrounding them was pulled back. Baines stood before them, a neutral expression on his face. "Bosses are coming. I've let you have your talk, now go back to your bed little weird one or we're all going to get in trouble."

Virginia gave the soldier a quizzical look. "You seem awfully nice for a soldier."

He shrugged. "Probably too nice. Now come on, before I lose my job." She walked back to her bed, pulling the curtain shut behind her. Baines looked at Stokely and said, "You behave all right? Don't talk back."

He pulled the curtain closed before going back to his post. Stokely could hear several people enter the room, their low murmurs gradually becoming distinguishable to him. "… and only a few weeks. You remember the last one. She seems worse, so you can expect probably two weeks at the most."

"And the third?"

"Hasn't shown any signs. Hopefully she's unaffected. It's already quite a bit of wasted effort. At least we've caught these two early. I'm going to keep monitors on them at all times. Try to collect as much data as possible. If we get lucky, we might figure out a way to better predict these problems in the future."

Stokely turned over his arm. The small silver monitor was still on his wrist, as well as another larger black one set closer to the crook of his elbow. He tried to pry them off with his fingernails but he couldn't get a grip on the metal.

Dr. Perseco pulled back the curtain surrounding Stokely's bed. Dr. Campbell stood next to her, an annoyed look on his crooked face. His eyes narrowed into slits as he said, "So. It seems you are more unusual than I originally thought."

Chapter 11 – The Crooked Man and the Devouring Bird

There was a crooked man and he walked a crooked mile

He stole a crooked sixpence from upon a crooked stile

He found a crooked bird, which ate a crooked mouse

And they all lived together in a little crooked house.

Sam sat, dejected, in her cell for two long days. She didn't see Stokely or Virginia and she wasn't brought back to the examination rooms with the other captive travelers. Mostly she lay on her bed, staring at the floor or the ceiling, it didn't really matter which since they were the same antiseptic white color.

On the third day, when the guards and doctors arrived to take the captives away for their daily examinations, her chaperones came as well. The doctor didn't seem annoyed or angry at Sam, despite the fact she felt sure she had broken his nose before. They silently led her back to the glass-walled room.

As soon as they opened the front of her cell the guards slapped metal cuffs around her wrists. Apparently, they now considered her dangerous.

The four of them walked to the same glass cubicle as before. The other doctors and travelers also went to their own little space. Sam looked around anxiously, but didn't see her friends anywhere. The two soldiers left the doctor and Sam alone. The doctor before her began quickly typing and swiping through holographic pictures floating in the air around him. Sam sat on the metal examination table, kicking her bare feet against the side with an impatient thump. The doctor stopped typing to look at her.

"What is your name?"

The question threw her off. He hadn't said a thing to her before and everyone else here only referred to her as AN14. She stared at him blankly.

"My name is Doctor Buroklammer, but you can call me Kurt. We are going to be spending a lot of time together, so we might as well call each other by our first names. I've told you mine, you tell me yours."

Something in the way he talked irked Sam, like a tourist talking down to someone they found interesting but beneath them. She couldn't place her finger on why she felt that way. She didn't answer him.

"Alright, well, if you don't say anything, I won't call you anything."

He smiled at her, as if this was some fun game. He rolled his chair over to her. In his hand he held a similar black, metal diamond she had watched a different doctor put on Stokely's chest a few days earlier.

"Alright, deal time. You cooperate with me and I'll give you two things. One, I won't make the guards come back in here. I don't think you want that. And two, I'll tell you what's up with your friends. Deal?"

She glared at him for a second before curtly nodding her head.

"I gotta hear you say it."

"Ok. Deal."

He smiled. "She speaks! Good. Now, I'm going to take those cuffs off, just don't break my nose again."

The two guards outside the door seemed to perk up when Kurt pulled off her handcuffs, alert and ready to rush in if she attacked him again. She gave them a cold stare as she rubbed the sore spots on her wrists.

"Sorry, need you to take your shirt off."

He turned around so she could take off her shirt, which seemed silly considering everyone could see everything through the glass walls anyway. When she finished getting partially undressed he neatly folded her shirt and put it on the small desk. For some reason this irked her even more. She crossed her arms over her bra, trying to cover herself as best she could.

"Lie back for me. This will pinch a bit. Hold still."

Four prongs slid out of the diamond, digging into Sam's skin. It stung for a moment, and then cold flooded her chest.

"Alright, that wasn't too bad, was it? This is my data gatherer. It'll keep an eye on you for me. Don't try and mess with it alright?"

He brought up more holoscreens and started flipping through them.

"Ok, I want you to go ahead and try to jump a foot to your left. Stay close to the present."

"Fuck you."

He smiled a small, half-cocked grin at her. "Look, I was telling the truth before. You do as I say and I'll tell you what's up with your friends. They are your friends, aren't they? The away team said it appeared as if you three were living together."

She stared at him. "You should know. You were spying on us."

Kurt laughed a bit. "The away team was watching you. They monitor information, apparent appearances of a single person in multiple time periods."

He stopped talking, staring at her calmly.

"Ok, enough talking, on to work. Go ahead. Jump just a foot to your left."

Sam crossed her arms in a resigned manner and prepared to jump. The smell of sawdust and oranges wafted through the air, although not as strong as normal. The shove in her chest also felt lighter than it should. She jumped, blinking out of the room for an instant, before getting snapped back on the opposite side of the examination table.

Kurt had gone back to looking at holopictures and typing in the air during Sam's jump. He smiled at her return. "Ah, that was quick. Might be a record."

She crossed her arms over her chest and stared at the floor. The room quieted for a few minutes. Finally the doctor spoke again. "Alright, again. This time go just a minute or two farther into the future. You only went forty seven seconds that first time."

And so it went for most of the day. Sam skipping small increments of time, Kurt recording his notes. Even though he didn't talk much he kept up his cheery disposition, which grated on Sam's nerves.

Finally, after what seemed to Sam an eternity, he stopped typing and turned to her.

"So, you've been quite cooperative today. And I promised to tell you what is going on with your friends. I figured you should hear it now, I know the guards sometimes talk when they shouldn't, so you'd find it out eventually."

He put the tips of his long fingers together and stared at her.

"They are in a special area, a medical unit if you will."

Sam jumped in. "Why? Are they sick? What did you do—"

He held up a hand and cut her off. "They aren't sick, as of right now. But they will die."

"What?! Why-"

"If you don't stop interrupting me I will call the guards in here."

Sam went silent, glaring at him with her hands balled into fists.

"Alright, as I was saying, they will die. We have had one other test subject die before, an elderly Belgian woman. As far as we can tell, there is something off with their brain structure which in the long term will render those collars lethal."

He watched Sam quietly. She stared at him, for once at a loss for words.

"We are making them comfortable, for now. After they are dead—or perhaps just before that—we will autopsy them both to try and find any abnormalities to prevent problems like this in the future."

"You mean to prevent the problems that you caused when you kidnapped us?"

He sighed. "We are doing good work here. This is, all of this," he gestured around with his hand, "is for the greater good. If a few people have to die to help humanity understand the nature of time and space, then so be it."

Sam snorted an angry, harsh laugh. "I don't believe that. You aren't sacrificing anything. Me and people *like* me are, against our will. This is a military facility. You aren't doing this for 'the greater good' you're doing it for a government. Is there a war on?"

Kurt shook his head. "This facility is run by a military arm, yes. And *some* of the scientists here probably really do want to support the war effort, but personally not me. It won't help anyway."

They stared at each other for a moment. Sam tentatively asked, "Which war?"

"The second Cold War. Do you know it?"

She nodded.

He went back to typing. "Yes, I imagine your kind would be very knowledgeable on wars. Wouldn't want to accidentally appear in the middle of a battlefield."

He stopped talking, eyes glazing over a bit, before tapping his wristband and speaking. "Yes, I'm done. Alright...yes. Ok I'll be there, I have a few questions for them."

He tapped his band again and turned to Sam. "I think that's enough for today. The guards will take you back to your cell."

As he got up to leave Sam saw him wave to someone. She turned and saw, to her utter confusion, Tony Eldridge walking towards them.

The man who had tried to murder her friends, tried to murder *her*, strolled calmly through the glass hallway next to Lieutenant Phago and four other people. Gone were the fancy suits, the only thing Sam knew him to wear. Instead he, like the other people with him, wore a black jumpsuit that reminded her of a wetsuit. Silver stripes ran the length of their arms and legs, and crisscrossed their torsos.

The guards startled Sam, coming into the room when she wasn't paying attention. They started to handcuff her again but the doctor stopped them.

"That won't be necessary."

Kurt went into the hall, walking away with Tony who, thankfully, hadn't noticed Sam. He was too busy talking with the Lieutenant. The guards pulled her roughly out of the room and back towards the hall that led to her cell.

On their way, several other guards ran past in a hurry. Baines, coming from the opposite direction, stopped to talk to Sam's guards.

"Hold up a minute. Their havin' trouble with that new arrival. Can't seem to knock him out."

Sam noticed Baines's split lip.

"Why don't they just shoot him?" one of the other guards asked.

"They did. Didn't take."

The others laughed and Baines looked over at Sam, giving her a quick wink.

Baines stopped focusing on the people around him. He tapped the band on his wrist and started talking, but not to them. "Oh, ok...Yeah, no not bad. He just busted my lip is all...Ok, I will."

He turned and started off down an unfamiliar hallway. "Adios."

Sam's guards seemed to have also gotten some new instructions. They led her quickly back to her cell. On the way she glimpsed the "new arrival" — a huge, hulking Asian man. Blood stained his clothes and he continually punched the glass front of his cell in frustration, his muscles rippling with each roar of frustration. He stopped momentarily to stare at Sam with unnatural silver eyes.

After the guards shoved Sam back into her cell and left, the dinner chime rang out. The compartment slid open to reveal a sandwich and a water bottle. Sam sat on her bed, took a bit of the food, and felt something unusual between the bread slices. She put the food down and as subtle as possible lifted up the top slice. A paper sat inside covered with only two words: DIVERSION TOMORROW.

She spent a good chunk of the night wondering what the writing meant and who wrote it. The most obvious person (she hoped) was herself or one of her friends. That was, of course, assuming they actually escaped from the lab. It could be the scientists themselves, trying to trick her. But to what end? She puzzled over it for hours before she finally drifted off to sleep.

The next day when the soldiers came to escort the captives to the examination rooms, Sam heard the guards arguing in hushed voices about who was in charge of the new arrival.

"I already had to deal with him. He almost broke my arm. You do him this time."

"Well he busted my lip, you don't hear me complaining about it. Lieutenant wants four of us on him anyway. Johnsee, Byrd, you help me with 'em. Barns, since you're so scared you can swap with Sky. Help with the kid."

Baines seemed to have some level of seniority over the other men. As Sam and her guards walked towards the exit door she saw the new guy's cell open. He cooperated at first, quietly shuffling down the hall, hands and ankles cuffed. But all at once he attacked his chaperones, hitting one square in the jaw, another in the temple. Those two went down hard. He used his immense strength to snap the chains on his cuffs. He grabbed Baines by the neck and slammed him to the floor before kicking the fourth guard down. It happened so fast Sam and her escorts barely reacted when he came at them. He slammed into her, wrapping his giant hands around her throat, pinning her to the ground. She gasped and clawed at his face to no avail. She might as well of been fighting with a statue. As her vision tunneled, she saw more soldiers rush in to subdue her attacker.

After what seemed like an eternity, they finally pried him off her by zapping him with a stun gun several times. Baines roughly pulled her up off the floor, bright flashing lights obstructed her vision as she tried to suck in a breath.

"Come on, I'm taking you to the medic."

She coughed and gasped the entire walk, leaning heavily on Baines for support. He led her to a room filled with beds partitioned off with curtains that hung from the ceiling. He gently sat her on a bed and went to knock on a door at the end of the room. The doctor Sam had seen with Stokely poked her head out.

"Yes, what is it?"

"Sorry Dr. Perseco, one of the subjects was attacked."

She came all the way into the medical room, peering at Sam. "Attacked? By who?"

"Another subject. That man we got yesterday."

"Oh, for god's sake. Doesn't anyone know how to keep order around here?"

She walked to Sam and pulled a pair of gloves out of her pocket. She gently tilted Sam's head.

"My, my look at you. Getting in fights on the playground, are we?"

She sprayed a bandage on the cut Sam hadn't noticed on her forehead.

The doctor turned to Baines, "Keep an eye on her. I'm going to get a blood sample from our new arrival. See if I can figure out those damn adaptive nanos."

The doctor left them. Baines turned to Sam, "Listen, I have to get something out of the back room. You sit tight, alright?"

He didn't wait for an answer before he strolled away to the room the doctor had come out of. Sam immediately ran back to the exit door, frantically tugging on the metal handle, but to no avail. It was locked tight. She wished desperately for her lock picking kit.

A quiet voice spoke out from one of the partitioned-off beds, "Hello?"

Sam froze.

The thin voice came from behind the curtain again, "Hello?"

Sam crept over to the bed and tentatively pulled back the curtain. On the mattress sat Stokely, ashen face with glazed eyes. Sam rushed to her friend and pulled him into a tight hug.

"Oh my god, I was so worried about you! Come on we have to go right now. The guard is in the other room. Where's Virginia?"

Stokely shook his head and weakly picked up a long silvery rope that looped tightly around his waist. It anchored somewhere under the bed.

"If you can get this undone, sure. Virginia's over there."

He spoke as he moved, slowly, like someone half asleep.

Sam walked to the bed he indicated. Virginia lay there, pale and still. A tube snaked from a machine up into her nose. Sam laid her hand on Virginia's forehead and said, "Hey, wake up."

She didn't stir. Sam turned back to Stokely.

"We have to get out of here."

Stokely didn't respond, only sat quietly watching her with tired, weary eyes.

Baines suddenly appeared, stepping quietly from behind the curtain. He wore a smirk on his face. "Thought I told you to stay put. Ah, don't worry, I'm not really mad. Listen, I need a favor from you."

"A favor?"

"Yeah, you heard of those, right? Do something to help me out. And maybe I'll do something to help you out too."

"What is it?"

He smiled. "Wear a contact."

She eyed him suspiciously. "Why?"

"Just need you too. No questions. I'll help you get that collar off if you do."

She was taken aback. "Why would you do that?"

"Tit for tat."

Sam looked over at Stokely. He didn't seem to be following their little conversation.

"No use asking him. They gave him enough drugs to knock out an elephant."

"Why? What's wrong with them?"

"Dunno."

She stood, arms crossed, biting her lip and thinking.

"Come on. Yes or no. Gotta decide now."

"How do I know I can trust you?"

"You don't. But I did let you talk with your friends, so that's something."

She looked at the glassy-eyed Stokely and unconscious Virginia.

"Ok. I'll do it."

Baines grinned broadly. "Excellent. Quick then, before anyone comes in here. That'd ruin our fun."

He pulled out a small bottle of liquid.

"You ever wear a contact computer before?"

She nodded.

"Good. Tip your head back."

She held still while he squeezed a drop onto her left eye. The liquid turned tacky after a second and sunk down. Sam saw a flash followed by a small red blinking light, just at the edge of her vision, indicating that the contact computer was coming online.

175

"Come on." He closed the curtains around her friends and grabbed her arm, leading her back to her bed.

About a minute later, Dr. Perseco walked back into the room. She held in her hand several small vials of blood.

"Thank you Baines, you can go now. Take her back to her cell for the rest of today."

Baines nodded. As they left, a man wearing overalls and an orange vest walked past, stopping to speak with Baines.

"Hey, what's up with your phone?"

Baines confusedly tapped the band strapped to his wrist. "Nothing. Why?"

"I've pinged you like three times. The cameras in the med are down. You were just there, weren't you?"

He nodded. "Yeah, nothing going on."

The man tapped his chin and made a small hurm noise. "Seems like something's been on the fritz every other day lately. Maybe this place isn't as protected from the flares as it's supposed to be."

Baines laughed. "Don't be a conspiracy nut. They aren't even gonna be that strong this cycle. If anything is going to knock out power, it's going to be something from the Moon Colony."

The man shrugged. "Probably just a coincidence then."

He walked into the med room, the doors shutting quietly behind him.

As Baines brought Sam back to her cell she overheard several soldiers talking about solar flares and the moon colonies. Opinions seemed to be divided as to which was a more serious threat. Sam already knew neither ended up causing any real problems, but she certainly wasn't going to waylay their fears by telling them that.

After a few hours of doing nothing but worrying and watching soldiers walking endlessly back and forth in front of her cell, Dr. Kurt came to check on her. He gave her a short examination, shining a light in her eyes and asking how she felt.

"I'm fine."

He nodded. "Yeah, you're pretty tough, aren't you? Dr. Perseco wants you to stay put today."

Sam looked out the glass for a second and saw the soldiers walking around. A question occurred to her. "Hey, those guys in black suits—do you know them?"

Kurt shrugged. "The away team? Sure. They're the ones who find and collect time displaced persons for us."

"You mean kidnap?"

He ignored her remark. "Why are you interested?"

"Um, no reason. Just a question."

He eyed her suspiciously. "Have you seen one of them before?"

Sam thought about Tony wrestling her onto a table and tying her down. She thought about him shooting Virginia in the face and trying to shoot Stokely in the head.

"No. What's up with the light-up suits?"

Kurt smiled. "Those are their time machines."

It clicked in Sam's mind. Tony wasn't really a traveler like them. He just impersonated one.

The doctor kept talking. "An adequate piece of tech."

"Must be a dangerous job."

He shrugged. "Yes, I imagine. The mechanics of the suits aren't overly sophisticated yet. We've lost a few, never recovered the bodies."

The doctor stood up. "Well, you rest up today. We will hold off on work until tomorrow."

He smiled and waved as he left. Sam wanted to punch him in his smarmy face. Again.

She spent the rest of the day nervously lying on her bed. She would have paced around the tiny room, but she worried her behavior might attract attention. Her thoughts drifted back to the note she had received. Had the fight earlier been the diversion? Was Baines involved? Or was the computer he'd put in her eye related to something else?

After a fitful, restless night the guards took Sam back to the examination room. Kurt acted cheery as usual. While they worked, Sam also kept an eye on her fellow captives. The young red-haired girl sat as far from her Doctor as possible, scrunched at the end of the examination table. Her skips through time were almost as short as Sam's, only going a few minutes. The tattooed man traveled in quite the opposite fashion. In the two hours Sam observed him, he disappeared and reappeared only twice. It made Sam think of Adja and her long sojourns in time.

The third captive she watched, a portly middle-aged man, traveled like clockwork. He skipped in what Sam guessed to be almost perfect ten-minute intervals. She wondered how someone could be so consistent almost every time.

Several of the guards stopped their general patrols of the halls, instead huddling near the back wall and talking amongst themselves. They looked worried. Kurt didn't notice, but a few of the other doctors did. Several people in the room started tapping their wristbands and speaking.

Kurt stopped typing in the air, tapping his own wristband, and started talking. "Yes, what is it?...What? No, that's ridiculous... No it isn't, you must be mistaken... NO! We aren't—"

Who ever he was talking to cut him off. He sat for a few seconds, obviously fuming, arms crossed over his skinny chest.

"What's wrong?"

He sighed and rubbed his forehead. "Those idiots think we're under attack. We're going into lockdown."

"Under attack? By who?"

"We *aren't* under attack. They think it's the Moon Colony. It's probably just a power outage or something."

He sounded so confident when he said it.

"How do you know that?"

He didn't pay her any attention, watching as several soldiers ran to the exit door, back towards the holding cells.

She said a little louder this time, "How do you know that?"

He turned to her. "Know what?"

"That we aren't under attack. How do you know?"

He waved his hand dismissively. "Another test subject told me how this ridiculous war ends. No actual fighting, just a lot of posturing."

Lieutenant Colonel Phago walked out of a door at the back of the hall. She was breathing heavily as three long scratch marks dribbled blood down her face. She looked around wildly before settling her eyes on Sam. She walked over to their small room and yanked the door open.

"You two, come with me. Now."

Before the doctor could say anything she turned and walked back through the same door she had come in. Doctor Kurt glared at Sam as if she had caused the trouble.

They followed the Lieutenant to an area Sam had never been before.

A long, grey hall lined with black doors that were stamped with numbers. Everything here seemed hidden and enclosed, opposite of the area the subjects occupied. A few doors stood propped open. Soldiers, obviously off duty, lay on bunk beds inside reading or chatting with each other. Everyone gave the trio curious looks as they walked past.

The three of them went into a room at the end of the hall. Inside sat a solid wood desk and leather chair. Guns of various sizes lined the wall behind the desk and several metal chairs lined the opposite wall. Sam surmised it was the Lieutenant's private quarters.

The Lieutenant sat down, gesturing for the other two to pull up chairs.

"AN14, have you ever been to this facility before?" As she talked she dabbed at the scratches on her face with a handkerchief.

Sam shook her head. "No."

The Lieutenant's eyes narrowed. "If you lie to me I'll put a bullet in you."

Doctor Kurt spoke up, "Lieutenant, what is this about?"

She pulled out her side arm and aimed it at his face. "Interrupt me again Kurt, and it'll be your end."

He looked taken aback.

She turned back to Sam. "You just appeared in our records room. You were screwing with our hard-drives. I want to know how you got in there and what you were doing."

Sam looked from her to the doctor and back. "It wasn't me, I've never been there. I don't know where it is, so I couldn't appear there."

The Lieutenant turned to the doctor. "Yes, I'm aware of the line of sight limitation you have. This other you informed me the good doctor here provided you with the schematics of our facility."

Doctor Kurt looked surprised and gave a nervous laugh. "That's outrageous!"

She smiled at him. "She also said you didn't give that information of your own volition. After your termination of employment here, in the very immediate future, right before your incarceration."

The silence in the room felt thick, wrapping around them.

Sam spoke up, quietly. "When's he incarcerated? Your time or his?"

The Lieutenant looked at her. "That is a very good question."

She turned back to the doctor. "Have you done something arrest worthy, Kurt?"

He sputtered a bit. "Of course not! This—this facility is legal. Our work here is legal!"

Sam spoke up. "It wouldn't be legal in the future. It's a crime to experiment on organic time travelers. You've probably broken a dozen laws from your own time, haven't you?"

His face reddened and he balled his hands into angry fists. "Pointless laws. There's so much we could learn from experimentation—so much more we could be doing if we understood how your brains work."

The Lieutenant re-holstered her gun and crossed her arms. Her gaze shifted from Sam to the doctor and back. "How much danger has he put this facility in by coming here?"

Sam shook her head. "He hasn't. Or not any more danger than you've caused by building the damn place. You should just shut it all down right now. Let us go before something really bad happens to you."

The Lieutenant's eyes narrowed into angry slits. "Is that a threat?"

Before Sam could answer someone urgently knocked at the door. Lieutenant Phago sighed as she stood up. "What now?"

Baines stood at the doorway, looking rather pale and concerned. "Ah—ma'am, ah. I'm sorry to bother you but we are having a slight emergency. Doctor Campbell is requesting you in his office."

She shook her head, annoyed. "Alright. Stay here and guard these two. If either of them tries anything, shoot them. Understood?"

He nodded. "Yes ma'am."

She left, slamming the door behind her. Sam felt like she had just survived a conversation with a hungry dragon.

Baines smiled at the two of them.

"Sam, I can't thank you enough. You've been very helpful."

The pair looked at him in confusion.

He took a step forward. "Now, Doctor Wąż, I've been looking for you for quite some time. Why don't you make this easy on both of us and don't put up a fuss, all right?"

Kurt stood up, jerking away from him. He looked wildly around, at Sam, at the locked entrance. His eyes fell to the weapons hanging on the wall. He dove for a gun but Baines was too fast for him.

The soldier lunged at him, pinning his arms behind his back. He wrapped a black shiny fabric around the doctor's forearms and hands. It immediately shrank, binding him, some kind of futuristic handcuff.

Baines smiled at Sam as he corralled the struggling doctor. "Thanks kid, you got me the evidence I needed to arrest him."

The doctor gave Sam a seething, hate filled look. "This is your fault. I'll make you pay for—"

Baines cut him off, slapping a piece of the handcuff material on his face. It contracted around his mouth, preventing him from speaking. "Shut up."

Someone knocked at the door, twice then once, sharp little taps.

"That'll be my ride then." Baines opened the door. The Asian captive who had previously attacked Sam filled most of the doorway. He grinned broadly at them. Sam stood up and backed toward the guns.

Baines held up his hands. "Woah, woah. It's ok, he's with me. He won't hurt you, I promise."

The man stepped into the room. "I didn't want to hurt her in the first place. That was your idea."

Baines smiled a bit sheepishly. "Yeah, it was my idea. Sorry about that. We needed a distraction so I could go snooping in the med room."

The Asian man grabbed the doctor's arm roughly. Kurt, or Wąż, tried uselessly to pull away from him. "I'll take him on ahead. Be back for you in a minute. Sorry again about the knock around girly."

He wrapped the doctor in his beefy arms. His silver eyes started glowing, light seeped out of his clothes, perfect little circles formed over his arms, legs, and torso. The pair blinked out of the room, like a candle flame going out.

Baines smiled at Sam's stunned expression. The man had still worn his collar, yet he could travel.

"He's not a traveler like you. I'm sure you're wondering, right? He was just pretending for our job."

"Worked that out on my own, thanks."

"Oh, well, anyway. Here."

He pulled out a familiar leather case. Sam's lock picking kit. "Found this in the personal effects closet. Don't think anything in there will get that collar off though, but I know where you can find the key."

Sam took the worn pouch. "Where?"

"That room at the back of the med room. The one I went in, remember? There's a retinal scan on one of the cabinets. That's the one you want."

She scowled at him. "You couldn't have gotten it for me?"

The Asian man appeared again.

"Time for me to go. To answer your questions, no. You told me how this would go down, so go complain to yourself about it."

The pair disappeared. Not for the first time, Sam couldn't help but feel annoyance and even anger at her older self for not providing more hints about her future. What had this all been about? Who were these people? Why the hell couldn't she just leave herself a simple note?

Sam tentatively opened the door and peered out. The hallway stood empty and quiet. Sam quickly pulled out her retina scan jammer ring and an electric skeleton key bracelet from her kit and put both on. She took a deep breath before darting into the hallway. She kept her eyes peeled for any straggling guards and was ready to duck into a room at any moment.

But she didn't encounter a single soul. She exited the grey hall, and reemerging in the white antiseptic area she knew she heard shouting coming from the examination rooms.

Choosing to ignore the commotion, she made her way to the med room. With a quick flash of her skeleton key, the door opened and she ran straight for the partitioned beds. Ripping away the curtains she found both her friends lying on the beds in the same state, horrible mirror images of each other. Stokely, too, now had a tube snaking into his nose and was completely motionless.

Sam ran for the door at the back, again flashing her skeleton key at a keypad. Large pieces of equipment crowded the room, and several metal tables and racks of surgical equipment lined one wall. At the back, she finally spotted what she needed: a retina scanner. The small round camera perched on a heavy black cabinet. She ran towards it, panic pressing her onwards, but as she neared it she stopped dead in her tracks.

In a glass-topped box was what remained of a human being. The chest had been cut open, exposing its still glistening organs. The brain and most of the brainstem sat in its own box beside to the body. All perfectly preserved.

But what was most shocking, was the familiar, aged face. Civic-Lee's hair, almost entirely white, was parted down the middle. A faint cut along the part marked where the organ that formerly made her *her* had been taken out. Thankfully, someone had thought to drape her lower half with a white sheet.

Sam laid her forehead against the case, resting her hands on the glass as she tried to blink back tears. Images of Lee flipping pancakes shaped like cactuses and birds, her blond hair in a braid down her back, flashing through her mind. She thought about Lee training her, helping her learn to appear between heartbeats.

There was a soft whoosh behind her as the door opened. She didn't turn around when she heard the tap of shoes on the floor nor at the faint click of a gun being cocked.

It wasn't until she heard the cold hiss of a voice from the Lieutenant that she bothered lifting her head. "Turn around slowly."

"You killed her." The voice that came out of Sam's mouth did not sound like her. It was small, dead, without any heft.

She turned to face the Lieutenant. Phago's hands were steady as she leveled her gun but Sam could see the naked panic in her eyes.

"Why? Why did you kill her? Why are you doing this?"

The Colonel lifted her chin and squared her shoulders a bit. "We are trying to win a war. Sacrifices are necessary."

Sam felt anger, hot and red, rising in her chest. "This wasn't a sacrifice. It was murder. You're kidnapping and torturing people for a war you can't win!"

Phago took a step towards her. "I am *confident* we will win. Now place your hands on your head and kneel on the floor."

As Sam slowly knelt to the ground, she could feel the gun trained on her. She eyed the black cabinet out of the corner of her eye, taunting her.

As the Lieutenant took another step a crackling noise filled the air behind her. Sam, in identical clothes but sans her collar, appeared behind Phago.

"Hey, bitch," she said, before switching off the lights. The Lieutenant fired off a shot at the duplicate but it wasn't fast enough. The other Sam had already disappeared.

The current Sam dove for the cabinet in the dark, frantically pressing her scan jammer ring against the camera's eye. The lock popped open and Sam yanked on the drawer. Fumbling inside, she found a small rod about as long as her hand. It felt cold and hard like metal. Sam grabbed it and ducked behind Lee's casket.

The Lieutenant fired several shots at her, each hitting the wall behind her. Sam held the rod up to her collar, not really knowing what to do with it. She moved it around, touching it to the back where the prongs were imbedded in her skin. Something beeped and clicked. A searing pain ripped down her back as the prongs pulled themselves out. She yanked the collar off and dropped it on the ground.

She suddenly felt light, like she'd been holding her breath and didn't know it.

She smelled sawdust and oranges, strong like it should be, and felt the shove to her chest.

Hello old friend, she thought to herself. She appeared a minute earlier, behind the Lieutenant.

"Hey, bitch," she said, just as she'd seen her double do before, flicking off the lights and disappearing in the blink of an eye.

She appeared a minute and a half later in the main medical room. The Lieutenant was halfway to Sam's friends' beds with her gun in hand. Sam ran at the Lieutenant, knocking her to the ground. The air whooshed out of Sam, but she ignored the searing need for air as they wrestled on the floor, each one fighting to gain the upper hand. Sam reached for the gun, but it was pulled just out of her grasp. A tremendous pop filled Sam's ears and a slicing pain coursed through her forearm. She'd been grazed by the bullet.

Sam jumped through time: about four seconds forward, and appeared between her friends as the Lieutenant was just getting to her feet. Sam held the rod up to Virginia and Stokley's collars in turn, yanking them off in a rush.

"Freeze!" the Lieutenant yelled. She stood in the middle of the room, breathing heavy, gun pointed. Ready for a second shot.

Sam froze for a second. She couldn't travel with a passenger, let alone two.

To her left, Virginia groaned. Out of the corner of her eye Sam could see her friend pulling at the cord in her nose in confusion.

"Don't touch them or I'll shoot them both."

Virginia sat up suddenly. She asked in a slow, slurred voice, "Where am I?"

She looked at Sam and tried getting off the bed. She tumbled to the floor, landing on all fours. In a quiet voice she said, "I want to go home."

Sam started to bend down to help her friend but the Lieutenant yelled again. "I told you—don't move!"

Virginia jerked her head around to look at the Lieutenant.

"You, on the floor. Get up. AN14, get her collar and put it back on her."

Virginia shakily got to her feet, grabbing the side of Stokely's bed to pull herself up.

Stokely made a choking noise, opening his eyes a sliver. Virginia put her hand on his. She reached behind her to grab Sam's arm with her other hand just as the Lieutenant's gun went off and the three of them disappeared.

Chapter 12 – At the Lake

The three friends appeared suddenly in the air over a lake, plunging into the icy water below. The cold shocked Sam, chilling her to the bone almost instantly. She kick wildly toward the surface, rays of sunlight danced around her underwater. She emerged from the water and took a giant gulp of air, wildly searching for her friends.

Virginia treaded water a short distance away. She seemed to be having trouble, dipping below the water periodically before resurfacing. A red cloud bloomed in the water around her.

Sam dove down into the murky gloom, frantically searching for Stokely. She spotted him far away—awake now and thrashing uselessly. He sank like a stone. She swam over to him, wrapping her non-injured arm around his waist and pulling him to the surface. He continued clawing at the water, nearly causing Sam to drop him.

"Stop fighting! I've got you! You're fine!" Sam yelled, but Stokely didn't seem to hear her.

Virginia had already begun to make her way to the shore. Sam followed, towing Stokely behind her, keeping her distance in case he tried to cling to her.

Relief washed over her once her feet finally touched the ground.

"Here, you can stand now." She almost let go of him, but thought better of it when she noticed how hard he was shaking.

She steadied him until they were on dry land. She turned back for Virginia, who had collapsed on all fours in the surf, small waves thrashing her.

Sam half-carried, half-dragged her farther up the shore. Stokely sat on the ground, coughing up lake water and shivering. Sam gingerly sat Virginia down next to him.

Virginia pressed her right hand against her stomach, blood oozing down her fingers. She held up her left arm and said, "It doesn't work. I think they turned it off."

The watch faces were frozen—the fingers locked in place.

Stokely pointed to Sam's arm, "You're bleeding."

It was true, blood ran freely down her arm where the Lieutenant had clipped her. "I'm fine," she replied.

Virginia held out her good hand, covered in blood, and stared at it stupidly. Sam kneeled next to her. "You need to keep pressure on it. Stokely, give me your shirt."

Stokely struggled to pull his shirt off, slow and clumsy so Sam helped him pull it over his head. She bunched up the fabric and pressed it against Virginia's abdomen. Worried, Sam scanned their surroundings: orange and red leafed trees were all that ringed the lake.

Where are we? When are we? Sam thought to herself.

She pulled Virginia up, leading her over to the tree line and laid her down on a blanket of fallen leaves. She turned back to Stokely, who was making his way slowly toward them. He stumbled and fell, his movements even more sluggish. Sam could feel the anxiety building in her chest as she went to him. He was cold to the touch, and although he no longer shivered, his eyes looked glassy.

Virginia's eyes were closed and her breath came in short, shallow gasps. Sam knelt next to her, touching her face gingerly.

"Virginia, wake up. You need to tell me where and when we are. I need to get help. Why didn't you take us home?"

She begrudgingly opened her eyes and barely said two words. "Virginia. Home."

"Yes, *you*. Tell me where you brought us. This *isn't* home!"

But she didn't answer Sam. Instead, she shut her eyes again.

Stokely spoke up in a slow slurred voice. "The state. She means the state, Sam."

"Ok. All right. You stay here with her. I'm going… I'm going to get help."

She knew the Pilchards owned a house in upstate New York in the nineties. They would be able to help if that was when they truly ended up. She'd been there before so she should be able to find her way back.

She took a deep breath and closed her eyes and...nothing.

It felt like something pressed against her, stopping her from traveling. With a sinking feeling she realized Virginia had taken them outside of Sam's traveling range.

Sam grabbed Virginia's shoulders and shook her a bit. "Wake up! You brought us too far! I can't jump here! Wake up!"

She didn't stir. Sam turned to Stokely. "Stokes, can you jump? Can you get help?"

He closed his eyes and leaned against a tree. "I'm tired."

Sam could feel a ball of panic forming in her stomach. "I know Stokes. But I need you to try to go somewhere. One of our houses, or the Pilchards, or Adja's, or something."

He opened his eyes and gave her a tired, dead stare. "I can't. Feels like something's stopping me. Not like the collar, something else."

Sam nodded. "Yeah, I felt that too. We're both out of our range. Question is, which direction?"

She looked around again. Only trees greeted her, no indication of the time period they had wound up in. Sam pulled off her own shirt and tied it over Virginia's wound to hold Stokely's shirt in place. The bleeding hadn't stopped.

"Is she ok?" Stokely asked in a small voice. He sat down.

"Her nanos don't seem to be working." Sam stood. "Ok. I'm going to walk a bit and see if I can figure when we are. If we're in the future I'll bring help."

"What if we're not?"

She took a deep breath, held it, and let it out slowly. "Well, I guess I'll figure it out then."

Stokely was in bad shape too, and probably needed medical attention as well. If they were too far in the past there wouldn't be anyone that could help.

Sam ran her hand over her own injured arm. The wound had already closed up, the skin was smooth under the caked on blood. So her nanos were still working.

She stood, shivering in just a sports bra and green scrub pants, and picked a direction to walk at random. "Stokely, you lie down. I'll be back soon."

Her friend nodded as he lay down next to Virginia.

She started jogging around the side of the lake. A river emptied into it on the far side. She decided to follow that upstream. People like to live near water, she reasoned, so hopefully she would find someone.

She jogged for twenty minutes, shivering and damp, before she saw smoke rising in the air at a slight curve in the river. She sped up, beseeching anyone or anything to be there. Around the bend sat a small, windowless log cabin, like something out of a picture book. Chickens scratched around a vegetable garden, white sheets hung on a laundry line. This was obviously the past. *Shit*.

The crunch of leaves underfoot alerted Sam to someone approaching. She ducked behind a tree, suddenly aware of her nearly naked state.

A man walked out of the tree line not far from her. He carried a bundle of dead rabbits in one hand and a rifle in the other. He wore a white shirt with a leather vest and black pants. A woman in a long, light blue dress came out of the cabin and kissed the man.

He hung the rabbits on a nail and leaned his rifle up against the house before the pair went inside.

Sam crept quickly and quietly over to the sheet hanging on the line and pulled several off. She paused for a moment before also grabbing the rifle.

She hurried back to her friends as fast as her legs would carry her. When she neared where Stokely and Virginia lay, Sam stopped short.

Two figures in black skintight suits were walking around. An away team. Getting closer she saw a man with a port wine stain on his cheek and a blond haired woman, neither of whom she recognized. They both tended to Virginia. They had already put another collar on her and they had replaced her makeshift bandages with real ones. Stokely lay quietly next to them, also collared.

Sam dropped the sheets and leveled the rifle, yelling out, "Stop!"

Stokely jerked awake, and the man above him moved to grab him, while the woman made to grab Virginia. Sam fired off a shot that went wide, hitting a nearby tree. But it stopped the away team's retreat. As Sam dropped the rifle and started running towards her friends, the man whipped out a knife similar to the one Sam had seen Virginia steal back at the military facility.

He hurled it at Sam, lodging it just under her right collarbone. Red blood bloomed and ran down her chest. She fell to the ground, clutching the handle of the knife, pain flaring in her body.

The woman's suit had begun to glow, the grey stripes blinking on. Before she could grab Virginia, the tempusnaut, opened her eyes, dragging herself away from the woman, and vanished.

The man turned back to Stokely, arms outstretched. Sam scrambled to the fallen gun, cocked it, and pulled the trigger. She hit the man in the dead center of his chest. Everything slowed around them, the man's mouth opening and closing in surprise before he crumpled to the ground and didn't move.

The woman hadn't moved, and stared stunned at where Virginia had been moments before. Sam gritted her teeth and wrenched the knife out of her chest. She hissed in pain and then hurled the bloody knife at the woman. It hit her in the leg, slicing through the suit and her thigh. She screamed once, a high angry note, before diving for Stokely. They wrestled for a second before they too vanished.

Sam ran to where her companions had been only a few seconds before.

"Stokely! Virginia!" she screamed.

But it was useless, of course. They were gone.

Prologue 2

Virginia awoke to the sound of her aunt singing and the chickens clucking. Thin light streamed in through the small window of her attic room. She buried herself under her quilt, momentarily delaying stepping into the chill outside her little cocoon. The aroma of bread wafted through the small cabin. Gentle singing from her aunt drifted up to her from below. Time to start the comfortably predictable day.

Virginia crawled out of her bed and dressed quickly in her simple dress. She ran a brush through her long brown hair before pinning it up in a bun. She placed the brush gently on her dresser; it was one of her most prized possessions, originally belonging to her mother. The only other item on her dresser was a framed photo of her mother, the only one ever taken.

Virginia ran her hand over the frame. In the image, her mother was laying in bed wearing her Sunday best, eyes closed. Someone had tied a ribbon in her hair. Her aunt had told her they had tried to put Virginia in her mother's slack arms, but she wouldn't stop crying long enough for the photographer to take the picture.

In the small kitchen, her aunt was tending to the fire. She smiled as Virginia was shimmying down the ladder and gave her niece a small peck on the cheek. She frowned a bit before laying her hand on Virginia's forehead.

"You still feel a bit warm, Vinny. I don't think you should be up yet."

Virginia tied her apron on. She loved her aunt, but disliked how much she still treated her like a child. "I'm fine Aunt Ida. I feel much better now. And I need to work tonight; Thomas said there would be another group coming through."

Her aunt nodded. "Yes, he stopped in last night after you were asleep. Apparently there is a baby with them. Your uncle wants you to give the child a few drops of morphine to keep it quiet during the day. There was a group found last week in Harpers Ferry because someone heard a baby crying in a cellar. I'll give you some sweet milk to mix with it before you leave. "

Virginia could still remember the bitter taste of the morphine she'd been given the past few days while she was sick. She knew the child would not be making any noise.

She and her aunt prepared breakfast: ash cakes, scrambled eggs, bacon, and beet root coffee cooked over the fire.

Her uncle James came in the house just as they were setting everything on the table. A chill from the fall air followed him into the cabin. Thankfully, the small space and lack of windows conserved heat during the cooler months, which were steadily approaching. As the narrow wooden door swung shut the smell of hay and manure wafted into the cabin. He kissed his wife and gave Virginia a hug, lifting her into the air. She giggled as he put her down.

"You might be a woman now but you still weigh no more than a cat. Maybe we ought to keep you around a few more years, until you're no longer a bean pole."

Aunt Ida playfully whooped him over the head with her dishrag. "You stop teasing the poor child, you hear?"

He smiled and turned to his niece. "Your horse is anxious to be ridden. Feeling up for a ride into town today?"

She grinned at him as they filled their plates with food. "Yes, I would love to. I've finished Mary's wedding dress, she'll be wanting it."

Her aunt and uncle exchanged a small look. Virginia knew the pair had been having whispered conversations late in the evening the past few weeks, when they thought she slept. She both did and did not want to find out what the look was about.

Aunt Ida said, "We were thinking you might wear your Sunday dress. It does look so lovely on you."

"Why? I'm just going to dirty it up."

"Well the Pentecosts invited you and your uncle to dinner with them. Their boy Reuben will be there. He's a mighty fine young man. The whole family is in agreement with the secession from Virginia."

Virginia pushed her food around her plate and stayed silent.

Her uncle interjected, "He's already running his father's store. One day it will be his. We just want you to talk with him a bit, nothing is set in stone."

She nodded. She knew what they wanted, of course. She would be seventeen in three weeks time. A good age to be married and Reuben was, in their eyes, a good man to marry.

The thought of it made her feel stifled, as if the world was pressing in on her. She wanted to jump on her horse and ride a million miles to the ocean. She wanted to go deer hunting in the crisp fall air. She wanted to work on the farm with her aunt and uncle until she was old and grey. Thinking of Reuben only brought up images of tight-laced corsets and stiff collars and rules too numerous to count.

After they finished eating, Aunt Ida washed up while Virginia helped her uncle with chores. There were horses that needed brushing and cows that needed milking. They pulled several fat orange pumpkins and a bushel of squash out of the garden. As the day began to warm up, the morning chill gave way to a pleasant September day. When the sun was overhead, even though she didn't want to, Virginia changed into her light blue Sunday dress and her aunt fixed a matching ribbon around her bun. Uncle James saddled up the horses and the pair headed into town.

It was an uneventful ride. They stopped to drop off Mary's dress first. The rumored reason for the hurried wedding was becoming more apparent by the day. Virginia hoped Mary's family was permitting the poor girl to wear a more comfortable side-lacing corset, despite the fact that it would allow the bump to show more. While her uncle was in the general store, Virginia went to the Whites manor to measure their daughter, Susana, for her baptism dress. The young girl was so excited she squirmed and danced around as

Virginia wrapped her measuring tape around Susana's tiny waist. From the front parlor room, Virginia could hear Mr. White talking with several other men from town. They were discussing the fighting, movements of the union troops and such. Apparently the soldiers had taken to burning barns and mills.

"Useless the whole of them. Can't fight worth a damn. Nothin but nigras and gal-boys and parlor soldiers."

She couldn't discern who was speaking, but it sent a prickle down her spine. There were no loyalists here.

"I say after a few seasons the bluebellies will have to surrender. It's only a matter of time before Britain declares for us. They would be nothing without our cotton."

The other men clamored in agreement. Virginia took the last of the measurements of the child and made her goodbyes.

After finishing their errands, Virginia and her uncle headed to the Pentecost's house. Mr. Pentecost had made most of his fortune in a salt mine years before and now ran several businesses in their town. His home was a large white manor with an enormous front porch. Red and white roses bloomed in the yard and crept up the side of the house.

A maid led them into the house. Although the Pentecosts were very wealthy, they did not own any slaves. They were led to the parlor to sit and talk before dinner was ready. Sunlight poured into the room through the large front windows, illuminating the portraits hung on the far wall. A lovely, upright piano sat in a corner and richly patterned rugs covered much of the floor. There was more furniture in just the parlor room than in the whole of Virginia's aunt and uncle's tiny cabin.

Mrs. Pentecost was wearing an incredibly fancy purple dress, unlike anything Virginia had ever owned. It had striking lace contrasts at the neck and wrists. Her hair was wrapped in a stylish matching hair net. Both Mr. Pentecost and Reuben were wearing silk vests over their collared shirts that made Uncle James look shabby in comparison.

They drank iced tea and made polite small talk. Virginia complimented them on their rose garden and Mrs. Pentecost asked how her dress making was going. When Virginia mentioned that she was having a harder time finding cloth the conversation turned, naturally, to the war. Mr. Pentecost said, "If it goes on much longer we're going to be raided by one army or another, mark my words. They can't feed their soldiers, and hungry soldiers will get food anyway they can, even if it means stealing from civilians."

Uncle James interjected, "I doubt the Union boys will. They're better prepared than the rebels."

Virginia timidly spoke up, "Mr. White said the Union soldiers are burning mills and barns. Why burn it instead of take what's there?"

Mr. Pentecost thoughtfully stroked his beard. "That is a very old war tactic, my dear. They probably can't carry everything they find on the farms. Burning the mills ensures no one from the confederacy will be using them for their own purposes."

There was a small pause in conversation. Reuben cleared his throat. "I must say, you look lovely in that dress, Vinny."

She blushed. "Thank you, Reuben."

The maid came in just then to let them know dinner was ready. The group filed into the dining room and sat at the large mahogany table. They were served fresh greens, smoked pork, fried apples, and bread. The food was much more spiced and flavorful than the plain fare Virginia was used to. During the whole meal Reuben, who was sitting across from Virginia, would steal glances at her with a small half smile on his face. It made her feel flustered and uncomfortable, so she tried to keep her eyes on her plate.

The whole encounter had a fake, structured feel to it. Everyone already knew how the play would end but they still watched it diligently.

After they had finished eating, they went out onto the front porch to sit. Mr. Pentecost offered to show Uncle James around the property and Mrs. Pentecost excused herself, claiming she needed to speak with the cook. When they were alone, Reuben scooted his chair closer to Virginia.

"I hope this isn't too forthright Virginia. My parents can be overbearing at times. They think you are a very fine young woman," He placed his hand on hers, "As do I."

Virginia was quiet. She didn't know how to respond to him. Stretched out in front of her, she imagined, was a life being neatly organized *for* her and yet without her. She began to feel faint, as if all the air had fled from her lungs.

She stood up quickly and stammered, "I, um—I just need some air. Please excuse me a moment."

She stumbled down the stairs of the porch and turned to follow the pebbled path to the side of the house. She sat down on a bench set amongst a large cluster of sunflowers. Sitting with her head in her hands, she could hear the front door open and close. The murmured voices on the porch drifted down to her secluded spot.

"…. my fault. I was too direct with her. I'm sorry I will go and talk with her."

That was Reuben.

Uncle James answered him, "No, no. She was ill this past week. My Ida wanted her to stay in bed but Virginia insisted she was well. I'll go check on her."

His boots stomped down the stairs and crunched on the path.

"Vinny?"

She rose off the bench. "I'm here Uncle. I'm sorry, I was feeling a bit faint."

Uncle James placed his hand on her forehead. "You feel a bit warm. We should go home; I think you still need bed rest."

She could tell from the look in his eyes he wanted to say something else, but he obviously didn't want the Pentecosts to hear.

As they headed back to the porch to say their goodbyes, Virginia's vision tunneled. She could hear a great whooshing sound, like a river, as she fainted. She couldn't tell how much time had passed when she groggily opened her eyes. Uncle James and Reuben were bending over her with concerned looks on their faces. Mrs. Pentecosts was standing anxiously watching them, wringing her hands. Someone had placed something soft beneath her head.

"I'm alright. I'm sorry I don't know what came over me."

She sat up slowly, holding onto Uncle James's arm. She turned to see the pillow under her head was actually Reuben's silk vest.

"Reuben, you dirtied your vest."

He laughed. "Your comfort is of more importance to me than some clothing. Although to be sure, I thought you would need it longer. You woke before my father could return with the smelling salts."

She smiled at him. "Thank you. I'm sorry to trouble you."

He shook his head. "Not at all."

Mr. Pentecost appeared then with the smelling salts in hand. "Ah, it appears I'm too late with this. How are you feeling dear?"

"I think I'm alright now, thank you." She slowly stood up. Everyone was staring at her and it was making her uncomfortable.

"Perhaps some tea before you go, it would put some color back in your cheeks."

She shook her head. "No. I'm alright now, thank you."

Their horses were brought to them and they saddled up to head home. The ride felt longer than it should to Virginia. She was tired, much more than she should have been. Several times she half-way nodded off and almost slipped out of her saddle.

When they arrived back at the farm, her uncle helped her out of the saddle and had her sit on a haystack while he put the horses up. They found Aunt Ida in the house, mending a pair of Uncle James's trousers. When she was told how the dinner went, she immediately set about making tea for Virginia.

"I knew you weren't well enough," She said as she hung the cast iron tea kettle over the fire. "I never should have let you up today. You need more rest."

"I'm fine. I just got a little excitable that's all. Reuben was - Reuben and I were talking and it just, it made me nervous is all -"

Aunt Ida shook her head. "No, I want you to have some tea and a lie down."

Uncle James had pulled his banjo out and sat at the kitchen table tuning it. "I'll have to go meet Thomas myself then."

Virginia crossed her arms. "No. We decided I'm to fetch the runaways. If you get caught they might hang you."

Aunt Ida was busy filling a mug with dried Cinchona bark and a bit of sugar. She said with her head down, not looking at her family, "I'll go then."

Uncle James calmly plucked a few notes, the sound reverberating through the kitchen. "No you won't. You're in enough danger as is. I'll not have you running around these woods at night, alone."

Aunt Ida clicked her tongue at him. "I'm not any more helpless than anyone else. I'll be fine."

"Vinny can run if she needs to. And she can always claim to be sneaking off to meet a beau. You wouldn't be able to use that lie unless we want to start some gossip in town."

"I could say I'm just going to—"

He cut her off. "No. You will not."

He rarely made direct orders to his wife but when he did there was no arguing with him. Aunt Ida sighed as she filled the mug with hot water. She joined her family at the kitchen table. The smell of the bitter tea wafted over them as Uncle James picked his banjo. He plucked out a few songs before anyone said anything.

Aunt Ida spoke up first. "Alright Vinny. *If* you have a lie down. Otherwise your Uncle will go. Understood?"

Virginia nodded. "Yes ma'am."

She quietly sipped her tea while her uncle played his banjo and her aunt sang along. After washing up her mug, she climbed the stairs to her room and lay down. She could hear her aunt and uncle working out in the yard as she drifted off.

She slept fitfully, her dreams filled with shadows chasing her and crying children. She woke with a start, her heart racing and the blanket twisted around her. The sun was just beginning to set.

The kitchen was filled with the yeasty smell of the bread Aunt Ida was baking. Both she and Uncle James were quiet when Virginia came down the stairs. She suspected they had been talking about her and Reuben. She wanted to make them happy, but they were making her feel like a chess piece being moved around a board.

Aunt Ida made Virginia eat a hunk of bread and some salted ham before she would let her out of the house. Before leaving, she gave her a basket filled with sweet bread and a brown bottle with a cork stopper in the top. It was mostly a prop, something Virginia could claim she was bringing to her beau, but it was with sweet milk and morphine.

****

The walk through the darkened woods was quiet. Her footfalls crunching on the leaves sounded loud to her ears, even though she tried to step lightly. There were no birds singing or dogs barking. She had a shawl wrapped around her shoulders to keep out the evening chill but she still shivered a bit.

She was headed for the agreed upon meeting place, an old stone mill that had been abandoned years ago. It rested in the middle of the woods near a dried out creek bed.

She had just rounded a bend in the footpath when her attention was called to the sound of distant, murmuring voices. She stopped walking, straining to hear Thomas amongst the jumble of voices.

She was so focused on the group she didn't notice someone walking up behind her until it was too late.

Someone roughly grabbed her arm, spinning her around. She let out a gasp but didn't scream. It was a tall, thin, gangly looking man with a wild unkempt beard. With his fist around her wrist like a vice, he leaned in and flashed a grin at her—he was missing several teeth.

"What you doin' out this late little miss? On a late night errand?"

She could barely make any words come out. "I'm - I'm going to, to see my fiancé. He's expecting me, he's waiting up for me."

The man lightly brushed her cheek with his free hand. "See, I don't believe you. Towns quite a ways in the other direction. Only thing this way is a few Quaker farms. That's not where you're headed is it?"

Shelli Frew

Without waiting for her to answer, he turned and dragged her toward the voices. There were three other men, two Virginia recognized from town and another she didn't. They all had rifles. The man shoved her to the center of the group.

"Found her round the bend over yonder. I think she was listenin' to ya'll talkin'."

Johnny Boreson, a large blond man who worked at the local nail factory, stepped towards Virginia and squinted at her in the dim light. "You Ida Jerman's girl aren't ya? What's your name?"

The man who had caught her was still holding her arm tightly. Her heart was racing and she could barely breathe but she managed to say, "Virginia Jackson, sir."

"Jackson?"

"I'm her niece, sir. I'm an orphan."

He nodded. "Yes, I remember now. Your pa died in a mine collapse, didn't he? Well, what are you doing out here so late at night?"

The man holding her spoke up, "She says she was on her way to see her fiancé."

Johnny crossed his arms. "I hadn't heard you were engaged to be wed. Who's the lucky gent?"

"Reuben Pentecost."

"Seems that's something would of been talked about around town. How long ago was that decided?"

She could feel the falsehood unraveling like a ball of yarn. Lies never came easily to her. "It hasn't been finalized yet. My uncle and I left the Pentecost's house in a rush this afternoon and I felt compelled to apologize. I'm bringing Reuben some sweet bread and buttermilk."

209

"It's awfully late for a lovely lass such as yourself to be out. There's talk of dangerous folk out tonight, contrabands and such. No telling what they would do to a helpless young lady out wanderin' all alone."

The other men chuckled and grinned lecherously at her. She tried to pull her wrist from her captor's hand, but he held fast.

"I'll be fine on my own thank you."

"See I don't think you will be. It's a very long walk from here, might take you an hour to get there. Sit and wait with us a spell, another friend'll be bringing along some horses after while. We'll give you a ride into town."

Her mouth felt dry. She glanced down at her basket, her hand around the handle so tight her knuckles had gone white. An idea struck her.

"That's very kind of you. But I'm worried if I linger too long my buttermilk will spoil. Would you like it?"

With her free hand, she reached into her basket and drew out the bottle. One of the men snatched the bottle from Virginia's hand. He pulled the stopper out with his teeth and spit it on the ground before taking a long swig of the milk.

Virginia prayed he couldn't taste the bitter morphine.

He grinned and belched before handing the bottle to the other man Virginia didn't recognize. This fellow, a red head with a pock marked face, downed half of the bottle before offering it to the fourth man. This was Roger Grant, a furniture maker and drunk who was rumored to beat his wife. He refused the milk as did Johnny. The other two shrugged and finished the bottle between them, passing it back and forth until it was empty.

Aside from the tight hold on her arm, the men mostly ignored Virginia, their talk turning to the war. For a group who were obviously not soldiers, they were all very opinionated on what the armies should be doing. Virginia hoped the morphine would have an effect. After a few minutes it appeared to work. The thin man's grip on her arm loosened and he seemed to be having trouble holding his head up. Roger and Johnny seemed not to notice, instead they listened for approaching footsteps.

From somewhere deep in the woods there came the sound of a baby's cry and, in the same moment, the red head slumped to the ground. Virginia wrenched her arm from her captor's grasp before dropping her basket on the ground and bolting in the direction of the cry. She heard Roger and Johnny give chase behind her, shouting wildly into the night. The thin man tumbled to the ground, apparently succumbing to the morphine.

Virginia heard a commotion ahead, several people talking in hushed, panicked voices as well as a baby crying. She shouted at them, "Run! They've found you! They have rifle—"

Something hard struck her ribs, knocking her down.

Her breath left her and she sat dizzily on the ground gasping and clutching her stomach. Roger stood over her leering. He'd hit her with the butt of his gun. Fire flared in her ribs. Johnny ran ahead of them, after the group. Shouting seemed to be coming from everywhere. Virginia couldn't make out the words.

Roger pulled a knife from his belt and slid it along her dress, making a slit in the fabric from her collarbone to her belly button. She screamed and clawed at him, but he was too strong. He pinned her under him as he ripped off her dress. She only wore her simple white shift now, freezing in the night air. She could smell his breath, hot and reeking of old alcohol.

Somewhere far away a single gunshot rang out, the sound reverberating off the trees. It drew Roger's attention for a second. Virginia took the opportunity to rake her nails across his face, leaving ugly, red gashes behind. He howled in anger and smacked her across the face, splitting her lip. She felt blood trickle down her chin, as he wrapped his hands around her throat. A tingling sensation started in her hands and feet. Colors began to swirl in front of her eyes.

All at once, the world changed. She still hurt, was still on her back in her shift but now she lay on a thin blanket of snow. The trees were gone, as was Rodger and Johnny and anyone else. For a moment or two she lay gasping in the middle of a field, looking up at the night sky and the sun slowly peeking over the horizon. Then she blacked out.

****

Sometime later, she groggily opened her eyes. Her head felt foggy and her limbs were heavy. It took a long time for her eyes to focus and when her vision finally cleared, the first thing she saw was a ball of light coming out of a thin metal stick. The strange object sat on the table beside her. The light didn't flicker and she couldn't smell any fuel burning. As she reached out towards the light something tugged on her arm. A thin cord, attached to her arm by a needle. The cord was made of a very strange material, shiny and smooth but very light. The cord snaked up to a glass bottle filled with a clear liquid attached to long metal stand.

Virginia weakly pulled out the needle in her arm and sat up. Blood welled up where the needle had been and trickled down her arm. A blanket covered her and someone had changed her into a strange loose-fitting dress that didn't cover her arms or legs below the knee.

The room contained only sparse furnishings, with the bed, small bedside table, and a chair. Outside a window she saw only darkness. Just as she swung her legs over the side of the bed and wobbly got to her feet, a woman stuck her head in the door. She wore a white dress with sleeves that stopped before her elbow, an apron, and a funny white cap perched atop her blond hair. Virginia had never seen hair styled like hers before. Short, only coming to her ears and parted on the side like a man. The front looked the strangest, cut very short so it sat just above her eyes.

The woman smiled at her. "Good to see you've woken up. Oh my, you seem to have pulled out your IV."

The woman strolled over to Virginia and gently but firmly guided her back to the bed. "Now you stay right here, I just need to fetch the doctor."

The woman left and returned a minute later with a tray in her hands. A tall, handsome man wearing a long white coat accompanied her. He looked oddly familiar to Virginia, but she wasn't sure where she had seen him before.

The nurse was speaking. "…just woke up I think. She hasn't said anything but she did manage to pull out her IV."

The man nodded. He held a small thin book in his hands, which he peered at intently. "She's been given some painkillers. Broken rib it seems. I'm sure that's made her groggy. The police really want to speak with her, but I've told them she's too ill. If you see any around please come get me immediately."

"Yes, Doctor Pentecost."

The Doctor pulled the chair up to the bed and sat down. Out of his pocket came a small metal cylinder, similar to a fountain pen but without the nib. He pressed on the back and the tip began to glow brightly.

"I'm going to check your eyes now."

He brought the light towards her face. Virginia pulled away sharply, afraid of being burned. He looked at her in confusion.

"Come now dear, it won't hurt. You've been to the doctor before haven't you?" To show her it was safe he waved the light over his own hand. "See? Nothing to be afraid of."

The woman, fiddling with the cord that had previously been in Virginia's arm, spoke up. "Should I get an orderly to hold her, sir?"

"No, Nurse White, I don't think that will be necessary. She's just had a rough time of it. Perhaps after we're done here, we can get you a bit of food and then some more rest."

The doctor flashed the light in Virginia's eyes. He gently felt her pulse while looking at his wristwatch. Then he scribbled in his little book.

"Now dear I'm going to feel your throat. Tip your chin up if you could please."

He gently pressed his fingers against her neck. She gasped a bit. She hadn't realized how tender it felt, from where Roger had tried to strangle her. The doctor turned her head from side to side.

"Doesn't seem too bad. Should be healed up in no time. Now," He made a note in his book. "Would you tell me what happened?"

She stared at him, unmoving.

He frowned. "There weren't any footprints in the snow around you, so you must have been lying there before the snow started falling. You were found around seven a.m. and the snow began falling at around ten yesterday evening. You're lucky you didn't get frostbite."

The nurse now messed with something on the tray. Virginia remained still.

"We're going to put your IV back in now." He spoke very slowly, as if she were a simpleton. "You have malaria. Have you been traveling anywhere tropical recently?"

When she didn't answer him, he turned to the nurse's tray to pick up some cloth and began to clean the blood off Virginia's arm. When he was finished, he inserted the needle into her arm once more.

"Now I need you to leave this in. You need this medicine. Do you understand?"

Her eyes wide, she simply stared at him. He sighed. "Honey, I know you've had a fright, but I need to know you aren't going to pull this out again. Do you understand me?"

Very slowly, she nodded. He smiled and patted her head as if she were a child.

"Alright. Nurse White, if you could find something for her to eat. Liquids I think, or else something very soft. Her throat will probably be very sore for a few days."

The doctor left, followed shortly by the nurse. Virginia sat quietly, thinking. Trying to figure out what had happened. Trying to understand where she was. She worried about her Aunt and Uncle.

After a few minutes, the nurse returned with a tray of food.

"Dinner was a few hours ago, but I found something for you to eat. Are you feeling hungry?"

Virginia nodded at her. The nurse sat the tray containing cup of water, a mug of broth, and a bowl full of some strange-looking bright yellow jelly down on the bedside table. The nurse picked up the jelly to give her.

"Look, they had some jell-o left. Hope you like lemon." She smiled as she handed it to her, as if it were a sweet.

Virginia took the bowl and stared at it. There was neither bread to spread it on nor cooked oats to mix it with. Did the woman expect her to eat jelly or, what she had called it, jell-o, plain? She tentatively spooned some into her mouth. It had a smooth silky texture, sweet with just a hint of lemon. The bite wiggled on her tongue before falling to pieces. She smiled at the novel sensation and eagerly finished the whole bowl. After she drank the water and the broth, Nurse White told her to get some sleep and left.

Virginia lay awake for some time thinking before she finally nodded off. She dreamed vividly the whole night, dark shadow monsters and angry troops of men with torches chased her through dark woods. She awoke with a start, covered in sweat. A small touch of light bled into the room from the rising sun. When she turned her head from the window, a man standing in the room startled her. He wore dark blue pants and a blue button up shirt with a flat brimmed blue hat. He held a little book similar to the doctor's.

"Well, good morning. I'm officer MacAlister. I want to ask you a few questions if you're feeling up to it."

She figured he was a Union soldier of some sort. She wondered if the town had been taken.

"What is your name?"

She stared at him, silent.

"Honey I can't help catch this person if you don't help me. Can you tell me your name?"

Silence.

"Now we know someone attacked you. That's evident from your injuries. But there were no footprints near you. I need you to tell me whatever you can about your attacker."

He paused, obviously waiting for Virginia to speak. When she made no move, he continued.

"Do you remember anything? What he looked like? Any physical description at all."

Just then another nurse stuck her head in the door. She was a small, older woman; her lined face framed by a curtain of long, grey hair. She strolled in with her arms crossed and said in an annoyed voice to the officer, "What are you doing in here? Dr. Pentecost says that she's too traumatized to be talking with you right now. She needs her rest."

The officer closed his little book and turned to face the nurse. "I'm trying to conduct an investigation here. We need to catch whoever attacked her before they attack someone else. We also need to know who she is." He jerked his thumb towards her. "She isn't being cooperative though, hasn't said a word to me."

The nurse shook her head. "She hasn't said a word to anyone, which if you had bothered to ask someone, we could have told you. As I said before *she is traumatized*. One of the doctors will let the police know when she is well enough to talk."

"This is obstruction of a police investigation—"

The nurse cut him off. "She isn't going anywhere. And I doubt she would be much help to you right now. The doctor is only thinking about her best interest. If you want me to get an orderly to escort you out, I will."

Before leaving the room the officer gruffly said, "I'll be talking to my superiors. This is a very serious matter that needs to be dealt with."

The nurse wore a small smile on her lips. After the officer had left she quietly said to herself, "Good luck on that."

She walked over to Virginia. "Hello. Now, I know it's no use to tell you not to freak out, but I'll say it anyway 'cause I already did."

The nurse touched her arm, which started a strange shimmering all over her body. The wrinkles in her skin smoothed out, her hair darkened, the clothes shifted into something else; she changed entirely. She had Virginia's face: her high cheekbones, her dark eyes, the small scar just above her eyebrow. Her long brown hair hanging almost to her waist. It was Virginia's twin. No, more than that.

It *was* Virginia.

The double smiled at her, a big toothy mischievous grin. "How ya' doin' doll face? You look a bit banged up."

She displayed an air of confidence that Virginia never possessed in all her sixteen years. She wore men's pants rolled to the knee, a shirt that hardly covered her, and no shoes. Six wristwatches covered her left arm, all different colors.

"I know you won't believe anything I say. That's alright, I didn't either. It's gonna be confusing for a while. I'm you, so you can trust me. And to prove it to you—"

She leaned over and whispered in Virginia's ear. She told her a secret, the kind everyone has. A small private thought or feeling or deed everyone keeps locked inside themselves. Something that will never see the light of day and therefore can only be known by one's self. And although Virginia still didn't understand what had happened, didn't comprehend that she could have traveled through time of her own accord, she knew with absolute certainty that this was herself. That she would one day be this strange, assertive woman. And indeed one day, about fifty years' time from her perspective, the scene would play out in reverse, with her coming through the doorway and giving instructions to her younger, scared self. But for now, she was still the frightened one, alone and terrified, adrift in time.

The other her pulled something out of her pocket, a small yellow piece of paper, it seemed. She gently placed it on Virginia's arm. It sent a pleasant, tingling sensation throughout her entire body. "That'll make you well. Much more effective than the medicine they got now. The ribs'll heal on their own. Just don't go doin' nothin crazy 'til they're better, ok? I'm not gonna hang around with you too much now. It makes me feel bad. I'd say you should head for the west coast when you're feeling up to it. You'll like it out that way, I promise. And don't worry too much about Aunt Ida and Uncle James. They weren't hurt. That's all I'm telling you, I think an Into-the-Fire approach is best."

The double touched her hand to her forehead, as if tipping an invisible hat. "It'll be fine, don't worry. See you later."

She shimmered slightly, before disappearing entirely. Virginia stared at the space her double had previously occupied with wide eyes, her mouth hung limply open as she stared at the now empty air.

****

Acknowledgements

This book is dedicated to my weird, funny, talented, fantastic, and all around wonderful performance family. The clowns, the burlesque dancers, the singers, the jugglers, the fire spinners, the aerialists, the acrobats, the contortionist. Everyone one of you taught me just how perfectly fine it is to be a weirdo, to live a life I want, to not place myself in a box. Ya'll taught me that I'm just fine how I am, but that I should also always strive to better myself.

To all the friends I've made over the years at Pacific Tradewinds Hostel, Dave, Abby, Eiji, Brian, and Chris chief among them. This book is due in large part to my life experiences from my time with you all.

To my folks, both biological and step, thank you for never trying to make your weird kid normal.

To my brother Troy, boy am I glad you are as weird as me. Let's go get drunk and eat donuts. Lizzy can come too.

To my wonderful sister Shanna, thanks for always being there for me, for listening to me talk way too long about my book, for encouraging me, and being the best little big sister anyone could want. Miles, thanks for being the best nephew in the whole world. J, thank you so much for reading a first draft of this book and helping me edit it and for encouraging me to send it off.

And to Robert. The wonderful, amazing, hilarious, best friend anyone could ask for. Thank you for helping me edit the very rough first copy. Thank you for reading even the bits that were scary. Thank you for inside jokes about my spelling and your patience with me. This book would not exist without you. Now and forever, you are the best.

- Shelli

About the Author

Shelli Frew is a circus performer and bookworm originally from Virginia. She now lives in San Francisco with 12 roommates in a big, old, possibly haunted house. She's traveled to over a dozen countries and plans to add many more in the coming years. Before becoming a contortionist, she worked as a bookseller. *Time Sailors* is her first novel.